ACKNOWLEDGMENTS

Although this novel refers to the German occupation of France during the Second World War, the response of the French Resistance movement to that occupation, and the activities of Samuel Beckett within the Resistance, it is a work of fiction, and is not intended as a faithful historical account of those events. The novel is placed in a definite historical context, makes reference to real people, events, organizations and locales, and relies on certain historical and biographical realities to provide a sense of authenticity. For that I have consulted and paraphrased information from print and other media sources including *Vichy France and the Jews*, by Michael Marrus and Robert Paxton, *Nous étions des terroristes*, by Jean Garcin, *Les Enfants de la Liberté*, by Marc Levy, *A Village in the Vaucluse* by Lawrence Wylie, *Samuel Beckett* by Deirdre Baird, Martin Esslin's *Theatre of the Absurd*, Marcel Ophuls' documentary film, *Le*

5

Chagrin et la Pitié, Wikipedia's "Les Milles Prison Camp" website, Christian Jost's "Clipperton Island" website, and the Jewish Virtual Library's "Drancy Transit Camp" website. I have also reproduced a photo from this latter site. The novel contains explicit and implicit references to many of Samuel Beckett's works, including *Watt, Mercier and Camier, Murphy, How It Is, Endgame,* and *Waiting for Godot.* And each chapter begins with a quote from *All That Fall.*

Knowledgeable readers will recognize that several of the novel's characters, specifically Olivier and Claudine d'Anglade, Jacques and Joanne Friedland, Richard Rosendale, Martine Lenouet, Jean-Luc Saccard, and the protean Raymond Crosatier, earlier appeared in the 2003 novel *L'Art de Vivre: a Fable about Paris in the 1930s.* That novel's debt to Georges Perec therefore should be once again acknowledged.

I also recognize with gratitude research assistance from Andrew and Judson Schwartz, and especially from Charles Potter, who provided valuable bibliographic information and rights for two photos included in the novel, and who tried unsuccessfully to keep me historically accurate. Thanks to Michael Anderegg for many helpful editorial suggestions, to Vivian Wyllie for the rights to two of her photos, to Susan Poriss for her creative input, and to my father, whose subtle pressure for me to get this published before his 100th birthday helped advance the composition. Thanks to Lucy for her helpful reading and everything else.

—Paul Schwartz, Houston, March 2009

PREFACE

*"I suppose you wouldn't be in
need of a small load of dung?"*

Just after dawn on a Monday morning in early
June, Jean-Louis and Estelle Robert were not
alarmed to hear the sound of two cars pulling into
the interior courtyard of their small family farm
outside of Cavaillon in Southern France's Vaucluse
region. Jean-Louis watched calmly through the
latticed window as eight armed men piled out of the
cars. One of them pushed open the door of the
modest rustic dwelling, and he and two others, after
motioning Jean-Louis and Estelle towards two of
the more comfortable chairs around the large
dining table in the far corner of the dwelling's main
room, proceeded to tie them to the chairs, while two
other men scampered down into the fruit and
vegetable cellar and then emerged quickly with
sacks of grain and potatoes. Those two men then

disappeared into the henhouse and came out a minute later carrying four sacks bulging with squirming, squawking chickens, while another man led a full grown steer out of the barn and proceeded to load it onto a trailer attached to the back of one of their cars. Two of the men in the house rifled through the shelves in the pantry and stuffed canisters and jars of dry goods into a sack they had brought with them

The whole operation took no more than ten minutes. Not a word was spoken, until the very end when Jean-Louis Robert, still tied securely to his chair, proclaimed boldly as the three men remaining in the farmhouse made towards the door, "The loss of my steer, eight chickens, the potatoes, grain and dry goods will all set me back some three thousand francs." A swarthy man who appeared to be the leader of the marauding party nodded with a faint ironic smile on his lips, "OK. Here's your receipt." and left a slip of paper on the table: "We certify that we terrorized M. and Mme Robert and stole from them important quantities of produce and livestock this seventh day of June, 1943."

An hour later, a lone police vehicle came screeching into the courtyard, and Officer Jérôme

Lambert of the Cavaillon Gendarmerie, following up on an anonymous phone call, burst into the farmhouse to release the still bound couple. He recorded all of the details that the apparently traumatized couple could remember about the terrorist attack and the terrorists themselves, offered expressions of concern, and promised to find the thieves and restore their losses. The Roberts thanked the gendarme profusely, and escorted him back to his vehicle.

That evening, as Jean-Louis was preparing to spread some fertilizer around his melon patch, he noticed a bulging envelope tacked to the barn door, and was not surprised to find that it contained three thousand francs in new one hundred franc bills.

CHAPTER ONE

"Do you find anything bizarre
about my way of speaking?"

That same morning, just outside the village of Roussillon, about fifteen miles from the Robert farm, as the sun began to reach its midday height, a tall, thin man, who appeared to be in his mid 30s, and who had been at work tilling the rocky soil of a potato field for over two hours, stopped, walked to a muddy hillock, sat down silently, and sipped some still warm coffee poured carefully from an insulated bottle. He was quickly joined by another man of about the same age, who had not been working in the field, but who instead had set up a wooden easel fifty meters beyond it, facing the red ochre cliffs, which he had begun to reproduce in broad colorful outlines surmounted by feathery wisps of clouds on a newly stretched canvas. He pulled a tin cup from his pants pocket and held it out to the laborer who proceeded to fill it from his bottle.

The first man, the laborer, put down his own cup, tried with some difficulty to remove one of his boots, finally with great effort succeeded, and peered into it. The two smiled at each other, glanced around at the countryside, and the painter muttered, in an American accented English, "Charming spot, Sam!"

And it really was! The subtly shaded red and yellow ochre cliffs glowed under the rising sun and seemed to enhance the colors of everything surrounding them: the deep clear blue sky, the lighter blue of the hills on the hazy horizon, and the greening vegetation at the base of the cliffs. The two men's worn faded clothing seemed to pick up the glow, which gave to the men an artificial relief that made them appear as if they were superimposed on a painted backdrop.

The two men grinned again. The painter pulled out a carefully preserved pack of cigarettes which he offered to the laborer. The latter, after a look at the sky and a quick calculation, decided to forego the immediate pleasure, and conserve the rationed cigarette for the evening. The two men continued to sit for several long minutes, lost in their thoughts. About ten minutes later, after exchanging a silent look and gesture, they both returned to their work, the artist more enthusiastically than the laborer.

An hour later, a thin but persistent bell rang from the village five hundred meters above the hillock, and the two men gratefully put aside their tools and walked together towards the village.

The painter, his easel slung over his back and paints and brushes neatly packed in a leather case, turned to Sam the laborer, "How's your work going?"

Sam answered with a strong Irish accent: "About a third done with the weeding and tilling on this field."

"I mean the other work."

"You mean *Watt*."

"I mean the novel you're working on."

"Right, *Watt*."

"Huh?"

"The novel is called *Watt*, W-A-T-T, like the electrical unit or Sir James."

"Oh, sure. How's it going?"

"Well. Several lines per day. It comes to me as I'm working in the field, and I put them down on paper at night."

"And who is Watt?"

"Interesting question, Richard. I guess the easiest part of the definition is that he is an

Irishman. Uncharacteristically, though, he thinks a lot. He tries to understand things that most people don't pursue."

"Like what?"

"Well, what if I told you that Watt worked for a man named Mr. Knott and that Mr. Knott wanted his dinner leftovers to be given to a dog in the neighborhood? You would probably just accept the fact, and let your mind move on to other perhaps more interesting details of Watt's and Knott's lives. Well, not Mr. Watt. Watt wants to understand how the dog happens to be there to eat the leftovers, and for that, he needs to create an elaborate network involving the dog's owner, and his family, and a system for insuring that the dog is present when and only when there happen to be leftovers."

"And so he investigates all that?"

"No, he imagines it."

"Correctly?"

"Maybe. He at least creates a credible system."

As they talked, Richard and Sam climbed up past a row of partially dilapidated houses near the edge of the cliff overlooking the valley, some with their front doors opened unto modest rooms where families were gathering for the midday meal. They entered into a narrow cobblestone lane which climbed up into the village, passed a small line of shops—bakery, butcher shop, pharmacy, hardware store—and walked towards the village's central square with the church, the town hall, and the Hôtel de la Poste, from which the bell had emanated.

The hotel was a three story building colored with red ochre and sporting a recently painted decorative inn sign in the style of early English hostelleries. The sign featured a stage coach, presumably a mail coach, arriving in a cobblestone courtyard, and the words "Hôtel de la Poste" in blue gothic lettering. The exterior of the hotel was plain, but well maintained. A neat little garden in front had three tall budding rose stalks. In the middle of the high wall which continued the building façade along the village main street, there was a heavy wooden door which gave access to the hotel courtyard. Another wooden door in the façade opened to the reception desk, in back of which was a dining room, rustic-looking with visible beams, and crossed by two long tables and two smaller square ones, one of which was set in front of the fire.

The hotel was managed by Martine Lenouet, Richard's wife; she had prepared a tasty but thinnish potage, which she served with bread and local wine. They were joined for lunch by another couple, a man in a turtleneck sweater and coveralls, and a woman in a fashionable but faded dress, and by Sam's petite companion, Suzanne. They all sat down quickly and ate with appetite. Warmed by the potage and the wine, the conversation picked up a bit, in French. They talked about the weather, progress on the work in the field, their respective plans for the afternoon, and the latest news from that morning's Marseille and Avignon newspapers.

Martine looked at the clock as it approached one-thirty, opened up an armoire in the corner of the hotel dining room next to the fireplace, and removed some dishes and linens on the bottom shelf, uncovering a radio. As Martine turned a dial, the radio hummed, and eventually a staticky voice emerged, speaking in coded language. As the speaker prepared to repeat his message, the six listeners conferred briefly to ascertain whether they all agreed on the meaning of the information given, announcing the arrival location and time of a parachute drop to be made into the area the next day. When the broadcast and discussion were done, Jacques, the man in the turtleneck, kissed his wife Joanne, nodded to the other occupants of the room, went out, grabbed a bicycle from the courtyard, and set off out of town. Martine turned off the radio, and pushed it back into the recess of the armoire. The three women began clearing the table while Sam and Richard moved to the other square table, after removing a chessboard and pieces from the same armoire in which the radio was now once again hidden.

Sam and Richard began a slow deliberate game of chess, which, if necessary, they would finish later in the afternoon after returning for a while to the fields, and before dinner was served. After several minutes of play, Richard made a decisive move, and looked up with a playfully smug expression: "I think your three-game win streak is in jeopardy."

"I wouldn't be so confident if I were you. I don't think you fully appreciate the danger to which you have exposed your king's bishop."

Richard looked intently for a full minute, then partially suppressed a gasp and a groan. "I wonder if it is written into our genes that a painter and sculptor, preoccupied with composition, broad outlines, and dramatic flourishes, will repeatedly fall at chess to a writer obsessed with the intricate subtleties of thought and human motivation."

"While I don't think that the outcomes of our matches are fatally pre-ordained, it may be true that habits of mind play a role in our approaches to the game. What I find particularly intriguing, however, is the multitude of factors that contribute to each game's evolution, especially the factor of pure chance."

"Chess matches determined by chance?" asked Richard skeptically.

"Certainly less so than the throw of the dice for example, but the permutation of possible moves at any point early in a game, and their subsequent consequences, near term and far-reaching, are vast beyond, I believe, the capacity of any human brain to foresee all or even most of them. It is possible that I will see a bit further than you, but within the huge scale of permutations we are dealing with, the difference in our perceptions gives me only a very slight advantage."

"And where do you think your minuscule advantage comes from?"

"You mean my predisposition to calculate and appreciate the role of a few more permutations than you?"

"Yes."

"Hmm. I suppose it goes back to our first teachers, whether they were parents, siblings, or our formal teachers in the earliest grades of school. Probably some heredity too in all of that. My father was a surveyor, therefore by nature an individual preoccupied with the accuracy of measurement and the perfection of straight lines. And I do find analogous tendencies in my first reaction to any new situation. But then my verbal and philosophic training kicks in, and it has taught me to question, to disbelieve outright the Cartesian interpretations of reality."

Sam paused a minute, reflecting on his own words, then went on. "We are in the middle years of a century which I believe will ultimately be recognized as a time during which many long held beliefs concerning systems of scientific and rational observation were challenged. There is now much evidence that anything circumscribed within the certitude of a system is subject to error. Current science seems to encourage mistrust of systems. In the '20s, a German physicist, Werner Heisenberg, proved for example that classical theories of motion, based on principles of consistency and predictability, do not hold at the electron level. He calls his theory the uncertainty principle. Without fully understanding it, I am convinced!"

Richard looked back at the game for a few seconds and made a tentative, defensive move, before reflecting on his own environmental and genetic predispositions. "My father was a welder in a factory in Milwaukee, and I certainly learned from him a fascination with metal work. But I don't think there was anything genetic that led him to that career, just a job opportunity that presented itself to him, and the instinctive sacrifice of all personal ambition—of all personal interests—to the necessity of bringing home a weekly paycheck. I understood that at an early age, and, while admiring his sacrifice, I committed myself much more selfishly to devoting my life to something more personally fulfilling. I quite naturally adapted the welding skills I learned from him to the service of aesthetic expression. As an adolescent, I was already creating welded sculptures through which I expressed strange visions that not only had no practical value, but which no one else appeared to be able to understand. Certainly not my father. But there again his sacrificing nature intervened. He supported my enrollment in an art school in Milwaukee, and warmly approved my later decision to move to Paris and enroll in the beaux-arts academy."

"I admire your father, Richard, and think you learned much from him in addition to welding skills." Sam glanced back at the chess board, and made a move. "Check."

While Richard and Sam continued their chess game, the three women set about washing the dishes and glasses, and putting everything away. Joanne, the woman in the once fashionable dress, glanced repeatedly at the old mantel clock, which she would continue to do throughout the afternoon, while she waited nervously for her husband Jacques to return. They talked little, but in response to a question from Martine, Suzanne told them that she would be giving a music lesson that afternoon to young Marguerite Bonnelly. Shortly thereafter, she gathered her teaching materials and excused herself, leaving Martine and Joanne, who took up their knitting and their places by the still glowing embers of the fireplace.

Richard and Sam finished their chess game— Sam won again—and headed back to the field. Sam worked efficiently through the afternoon, removing rocks and weeds, smoothing the soil. He continued working for three and a half hours, rarely pausing, or even looking up. Richard painted, stopping often to think and stare, adding detail, texture and new colors to his landscape. Very conscious of the evolution of the light throughout the afternoon, he tried to retain mental images of the most pleasing combinations of shadow and light, and to record them on the canvas before they were lost. The afternoon wore on; as the sun began to descend into the valley, the two men looked at each other, nodded, and began to pack up their equipment for the walk back towards the village.

Sam glanced at Richard's canvas, "Looks to be nearly finished?"

Richard nodded. "Yes, nearly. You know, everything they've always said about the extraordinary natural light in this part of the world is true. It is fascinating, maddening, and truly inspiring. I'm impatient to finish one canvas, so I can move on to the next and capture another moment, another shade of yellow or red, another contrast between the sun revealed color and its shadowed counterpart. I used to think that landscape painting was an old-fashioned and irrelevant form, but the countryside here screams out to be painted, to be preserved and exhibited. Does any of it appear in *Watt*?"

"Not really. I can certainly see and appreciate what you see here. But I am not a painter. Watt's natural surroundings tend to be dreary and Irish. Besides, a lot of his world is nocturnal."

"Sam, when I create a painting or a sculpture, I try to express what I see and how I understand it, but always in the back of my mind is a thought for the others, those who will see my work and respond to it in some way, perhaps even purchase it, so that I will have enough money to buy some more paint, or some more bronze, with maybe a little left over for food. This has at times in my career been a preoccupation: what will the critics say about my work, how many art lovers will come to my exhibit? But I don't sense that in your approach to writing. I have read *Murphy*, Sam. And I can't help wondering for whom you wrote it."

Sam chuckled. "I am afraid that I write for myself first of all, to satisfy my need to express what I hear inside, and then, secondarily—and it is a very distant second—for a small group of knowledgeable friends, associates and fellow writers whose intelligence and judgment I respect."

"Like Mr. Joyce?"

"Like Mr. Joyce. Who incidentally has enjoyed a much wider reading audience than I would ever aspire to. *Murphy* and now *Watt* are not going to entertain or even interest a lot of people, obviously. They are far too idiosyncratic. Given all that, you will be amused to learn that I envision the possibility of one day writing for the theatre. There I obviously face a greater challenge: while it is possible to write books that no one will read, and they can still be objectively considered books, the problem with theatre is more complex. Can we still call a theatrical presentation that no one will watch a play?"

They re-entered the village and arrived at the hotel as the sun was setting. As they closed the hotel door behind them, both sensed immediately tension and anxiety in the look of Martine, who was seated in a corner of the reception area looking at the window. She turned as the two men entered, "It's Jacques. He hasn't come back yet." Richard didn't hesitate for a second, "I'll go look for him." He ran to the courtyard door, pushed it open, grabbed a bicycle, and headed back out into the countryside.

As evening turned to night, Martine, Suzanne, and Joanne sat working together in the small hotel kitchen to put dinner together, but their hearts were not in the task. All three kept looking at the clock, and looking down the street, waiting for Jacques to appear or for Richard with news of Jacques. Finally, Richard appeared, alone, and the look on his face did nothing to relieve the anxiety in their hearts. "Denounced, arrested, and taken off by the Gestapo." The eight words confirmed their worst fears. Joanne sobbed as Martine and Suzanne did their best to comfort her.

"We'll get him back!"

The words came from the table in the corner of the fireplace where Sam Beckett sat writing in a notebook.

Chapter Two

"Why do you not climb up on the crest of your manure and let yourself be carried along?"

Jacques Friedland woke up as a sliver of sunlight appeared on the floor of his cell in the prison camp at Les Milles. He could dimly make out the forms of the men sprawled on the straw covered concrete around him. Before he had time to interact with any of them, two guards appeared at the door with small loaves of bread, a jug of coffee and some tin mugs, all of which they left in a corner of the cell, before removing and replacing the filled chamber pots from the opposite corner. Jacques tried to make eye contact with one of the guards as he cut a diagonal across the cell, to see if he could discern anything in his look that might provide some information about what they could expect, but the guard kept his eyes intentionally downcast. Jacques muttered thanks anyway, and grabbed a loaf and a mug, which he filled, and then went back to his spot on the floor. The other prisoners did the same. Jacques heard some muffled conversation through which he discerned the words, "They're French, just like us." Jacques couldn't help thinking, "Not quite like us," but he had no real anger for the guards who were very young, and who had undoubtedly joined the Gendarmerie because they had no other options if they wanted to avoid been shipped off to forced labor in Germany. They didn't really understand what country they were serving. While sipping their weak coffee, the prisoners clustered in small groups and exchanged information.

The prisoner closest to Jacques, the one who had commented on the guards' nationality, was a young man from the village of Vauvenargues. His name was Joseph Leydet, and he dreamed of being an artist. He had ignored the call to forced labor, preferring to take to the woods with others like himself who lived off the land. Just the morning before, he had run into a German roadblock, and, unable to provide appropriate identification, was arrested and sent to the prison at Les Milles. He knew that the Germans were not particularly interested in punishing people like him who were guilty only of trying to avoid deportation for forced labor, and that the worse thing likely to happen to him was to be sent to a labor camp. He sympathized with Jacques, who had been denounced as a maquisard and was tagged with a Jewish surname. Leydet feared that Jacques would be deported, and then who knew what?

Jacques didn't bother to tell him about his conversation the previous day, just after his arrival at the prison, with the prison chaplain Father Marie-Benoît, and the possibility that his baptism certificate might gain his release. He didn't really believe it himself. There were bound to be too many questions about his connections over the past two years.

Following the declaration of war in 1939, the French government had initiated a policy of interning residents of Swiss, German or Austrian nationality living in southeastern France in a prison facility located in the village of Les Milles just outside of Aix-en-Provence. Many of the first victims of this persecution were anti-fascist German, Austrian, and Swiss artists and intellectuals who had sought refuge from Hitler's fascist Germany, including some well known artists—Hans Bellmer, Leo Marchutz, and Max Ernst, for example—who left elaborate murals with famous signatures on the walls of the prison. The camp began to receive a constant flow of Jewish detainees as the result of an agreement signed on January 20, 1942, in which the Vichy government pledged to arrest and intern 10,000 Jews living in the French Free Zone and turn them over to German occupying forces. In the course of the next two years, 2500 Jewish men, women and children were detained at Les Milles before being deported to Auschwitz by way of the Drancy camp outside of Paris. Conditions at the camp were particularly appalling. André Jean-Faure, inspector general of camps and internment centers for the Vichy government, following an inspection tour in the fall of 1942, noted in his report that at the camp in Les Milles, food and heat were serious problems. Inmates received a ration of only 150-200 grams of dried vegetables per day, and overcrowding had brought about the spread of lice and fleas. Several outbreaks of dysentery had been reported.

Time passed slowly for Jacques through the morning. There was a meager midday meal with dried vegetables and water. Then, perhaps an hour later, the doors opened, two guards came in, and, motioning to Jacques, told him to follow them. As he was led through the halls and out into the courtyard, a growing procession formed. Outside, they were marched towards the Les Milles train station, surrounded by a large number of armed police. Jacques guessed that there were at least 250 prisoners, and 50 guards. At the station, they stood in front of a cargo train as their names were called in alphabetical order. Jacques noticed that many of the prisoners were members of a single family, with Jewish surnames. As they piled into the train cars, there were muffled expressions of concern and dismay, as they realized there were no seats, and they were expected to sit on a thin layer of foul-smelling straw spread out on the floor of the cars. Chamber pots were placed at either end of the car as a gesture towards accommodating human needs.

The calling of names seemed to drag on for hours. The prisoners became increasingly agitated and fatigued, but the guards showed no signs of compassion or even interest. When some of the children or women tried to sit down to rest, they were curtly told to remain standing, and those who resisted were roughly shoved, and occasionally even poked with the ends of rifles. When all of the prisoners were aboard, the doors of the train were tightly closed, and minutes later, the cars jolted into motion. On the hill overlooking the train station a large group of family members and friends watched silently, sadly waving handkerchiefs at the departing train.

Jacques was placed with approximately two dozen other prisoners in a hot claustrophobic boxcar. Among those sprawling with him on the soiled straw on the floor of the train car were Jews, gypsies, and then some others whose identity was not clear. There were two guards in the car, both armed only with pistols, and Jacques wondered briefly about the possible effectiveness of a concerted attack, but the guards allowed no conversation, and Jacques, a loyal and effective follower in the Resistance, lacked resourcefulness and leadership ability. The hours passed silently, with prisoners making futile efforts to get comfortable and sleep some. There were no windows in the car, but the space between the roof of the car and the walls let in enough light so that Jacques could count his fellow travelers—twenty-seven—and size them up. He was relieved that there were no families with children in his car, as he had noticed several of them waiting with him at the station, and had found the sight heart-rending. His fellow travelers were all males, between the ages of eighteen and seventy, all wearing the clothes in which they had been arrested. Some were clearly farm laborers and tradesmen, others appeared to be well off merchants. Jacques thought he recognized one man as the owner of the jewelry store in Vence whom he had known when he lived there.

Jacques fell into a sullen resignation as the miles passed by. He could see occasional lights, a bit of sky, mountains at times, through the opening just below the roof. But he soon gave up trying to identify any landmarks. He felt that that the train was traveling slowly.

The train stopped three times as the night wore on. At the first stop, two new prisoners were pushed into the car with Jacques, and two more at the second stop. At the third stop, three new prisoners came into the car, along with a gendarme who replaced one of the guards who had accompanied them since Les Milles. It was several minutes after the train had started up again that Jacques happened to look up into the face of the new guard. For a full five seconds he stared dumbly, thinking he was hallucinating. The new guard in a gendarme uniform looked exactly like Félix Arnaud, the leader of the Roussillon maquis. As Jacques' mouth started to open in surprise, the guard's eyes moved sharply towards the prisoner who had just taken his place across from where Jacques was sitting. Jacques first noticed stamped on the sleeve of the prisoner the words, "Paris-Drancy," and then looking up, saw that it was Sam Beckett.

CHAPTER THREE

*"Sigh out a something something tale of
things. Done long ago and ill done."*

Félix Arnaud returned to the Hôtel de Maubeuge
near Paris's Gare du Nord just after noon, and
briefed Richard Rosendale on his successful
morning activities. They had nearly three hours
before their meeting with Olivier d'Anglade, so they
decided to have a quick lunch, then take a long walk
to the Île de la Cité where they were to meet him. The
café near the hotel where they had lunch was too
crowded to permit any serious conversation about
their plans. They leafed through the morning
Figaro, commenting ironically on the obviously
censored reports of fighting along the German-
Russian front. Arnaud had heard that the German
army was encountering fierce resistance, and being
forced from previously held positions in the
Leningrad region near Novgorod. There were

reports of as many as 40,000 German casualties. But the paper downplayed the action and implied that the Russian army was engaged in nothing more than harassment strategies against German held positions. It also appeared to exaggerate the effectiveness of German bombing raids aimed at the Russian fleet and Anglo-American supply ships near the ports of Leningrad and Cronstedt. And the paper contained no references to allied bombing raids made the night before against German held positions in the north of France near Saint-Omer.

The paper's domestic news of the day appeared to have been manipulated to encourage stoic resignation. There was a long front page story about a speech given by the Minister of Agriculture, Pierre Caziot, in Valence, in which he exhorted members of the regional agricultural council to increase their production, to help win what he called "the Bread War." Recognizing the daily hardships imposed by the country's economic isolation, he stressed the patriotic duty of the farming community to meet the nation's needs. Otherwise, the country would face the even greater hardships which would inevitably result from the mutinous environment festering within a hungry populace. "From hunger is born a despair which engenders disorder, which in turn would lead to communism and the horrors of civil strife." Another article further inside exhorted citizens to be patient with the newly imposed wine rationing, and tried to explain why there was a shortage within a country blessed with abundant grape fields (for example blaming the lack of imported copper sulfate).

An article in the entertainment section caught Richard's attention, a mixed review of the Comédie-Française's new production of *Hamlet*, starring Jean-Louis Barrault. The reviewer found much to criticize in the production, but praised Barrault's solid, authentic performance. Richard mentioned to Arnaud that he had met Barrault during his Paris years, when the young actor was performing at the Théâtre de Marigny, and was delighted to learn of his growing success. He wondered aloud if they might have time that evening to see the production.

At about one-thirty, the two set out towards the Île de la Cité for their three o'clock meeting with Olivier d'Anglade. They walked down the Boulevard de Magenta to the intersection with the Boulevard de Sébastopol, which they took to the Seine. As they strolled along the boulevards, they looked, mostly in vain, for signs that France was suffering under an abhorrent occupation, and that a fierce struggle was underway for its deliverance. The only consistent sign of distress was the paucity of articles in the windows of most shops, especially food shops. But people seemed to be going about their business normally, perhaps walking a bit more rapidly, and no one seemed to be smiling. However, as Richard commented to Arnaud, even in the best of times, Parisians rarely smiled. Three times in the course of their walk they encountered a small group of German soldiers, who also walked quickly without smiling, and without acknowledging them. The soldiers appeared more like awkward, unwelcome visitors than triumphant occupiers. At one point they passed an elderly Jewish couple with yellow stars sewn on their coats.

Arriving a bit early on the Cité, Richard and Arnaud wandered towards Notre Dame Cathedral, and walked inside. The morning's heavy cloud cover had dissipated, and bright sunlight now illuminated the stained glass windows. Several worshippers knelt at altars around the edges of the nave. It was eerily silent. They sat without talking in a dimly lit corner, waiting for their three o'clock meeting with d'Anglade.

The black Citroen was waiting for them at the curb just outside the Sainte Chappelle. They climbed in. Olivier d'Anglade greeted them warmly, "Good afternoon! I have informed my ministry colleagues that I will be spending the latter part of the afternoon showing my American and Mexican friends that Paris is still the most beautiful city in the world." He then handed them an envelope and an official looking briefcase. "The envelope contains documents which must not leave the car. Therefore, both of you need to read and memorize the information they contain about the train, its route and anticipated stops, while I drive around the city. They describe what we have learned from several reliable sources about the physical structure of the twenty-four train cars making up the deportation train leaving tomorrow from Drancy for camps in Poland, its precise schedule, including locations and times of all intermediate stops, as well as information about the deployment of members of the eastern region Resistance units. Félix, you will need to find a way to communicate that information to Beckett. Richard, there is a ministry ID and a pass which will get you into the Drancy train station tomorrow for the departure, as an official ministry observer. You will be amused to see that both are in the name of your old friend Raymond Crosatier (who incidentally is doing valuable Resistance work in London). You and Félix need to agree on a meeting place within the station. The brief case contains a change of clothes for you, and a gun. I have received this morning confirmation that the eastern region Resistance network will be in place in the woods outside of Metz; and we are certain now that the train will cross the border into Germany through Mulhouse." With that, d'Anglade set out crisscrossing Paris for more than an hour while Richard and Arnaud absorbed the detailed information in the envelope. At four-thirty, the car stopped in front of the Hôtel de Maubeuge, and the two men got out and went up to their room.

When they got to the room, Arnaud packed up his gendarme uniform, and headed out the door, "I need to get back to the prison and talk to Beckett. Why don't we meet just before eight at the Comédie-Française? I think I can get back in time, and I would like to see your friend perform."

Richard Rosendale napped briefly, dined lightly at a café, and then set out on the métro to the Palais Royal, arriving at seven-thirty. Hard times and the early curfew had taken its toll on theatre attendance, and, as he had expected, he had no trouble buying two last minute seats for the performance. Arnaud arrived in the theatre lobby fifteen minutes later, spotted Richard, and gave a discreet thumbs up to signal that he had succeeded in finding and briefing Beckett (in fact he had condensed all of the information into a ten minute monologue that he had dictated twice to Beckett in the course of a simulated interrogation in the prison). They took their seats amid a fairly sparse crowd composed of elegant, wealthy theatre patrons, German officers, and several groups of students and professors.

The production was totally engrossing. Barrault *was* Hamlet, at times brooding and neurotic, and alternately playful, thoughtful, coarse, mocking and mad. Richard was disturbed at the scene in which he brutally pushes Ophelia to the ground, and equally disturbed by his overtly sensual relation to his mother. At the end, Richard and Arnaud applauding wildly while the rest of the more subdued Parisian crowd acknowledged with far more restraint the remarkable performance they had seen, attracted Barrault's attention. He looked in their direction, then seemed to wink.

Richard turned to Arnaud, "Let's go find him." Arnaud followed Richard down a hall off the lobby to a bank of elevators. Richard told the guard that M. Barrault was expecting them, and the guard believed him. The elevator took them up to the dressing room floor. Richard headed down the hall unsure which way to turn or on which door to knock, when all of a sudden he heard a squawking voice call out dramatically behind him, "No bird sellers allowed on this floor, even if the birds are bronze and artsy!" It was Barrault who kissed him on both cheeks and enthusiastically ushered both of them into his dressing room.

"Richard, how good of you to come see our *Hamlet*! The last time I saw you was in 1937, when you were producing strange bronze bird statues. Then I heard rumors you had died. But, I guess the rumors were exaggerated!"

"Not dead, just moved south, to Provence."

"What brings you back?"

"I heard that there was an amazing *Hamlet* at the Comédie-Française, and that rumor turns out to be not at all exaggerated."

"That's very flattering Richard, but a play is just a play. What's up?"

"My friend Félix and I are trying to help out a couple of friends who are in a little trouble. You might know one of them, Samuel Beckett?"

"I don't think so. Who is he?"

"An Irish writer. I know you would like him and his work."

"I'll remember the name. Once this whorish war is over, maybe we can do some real theatre."

"*Hamlet*'s not real?"

"Of course it is, but when you can only do plays that the Germans approve, it all seems less fun. Actually, it is a bit of a miracle that they let us perform *Hamlet*. The play is after all English, and the translation we are using is by André Gide! And then I just have to guess that the censors really don't understand what *Hamlet* is all about. But we're going to be working soon on an exciting cinema project with Marcel Carné and Jacques Prévert, behind closed doors."

"What's it about?"

"Well, I haven't seen the whole script yet; it is basically a love story, but set within the world of the mid nineteenth century Parisian theatre."

"Any roles for a lousy actor with an American accent?"

"Probably not, but we could maybe use an assistant set designer; a lot of the action takes place in a bar with bird motifs."

"Sounds promising. Can we buy you a drink?"

"You certainly can. Let's meet Madeleine

downstairs, and we'll see what's open."

Barrault dressed quickly, and they took the elevator back down to the lobby where Madeleine Renaud greeted them enthusiastically. She had found a night club, le Kilt, which had semi-official approval to remain open after the curfew on the condition of offering drinks to officers of the Reich. It was noisy, crowded, smoky, and awkward, at least for the two active members of the French Resistance who found themselves shoulder to shoulder with German army officers. Barrault's celebrity status was a satisfactory shield for his American and Mexican guests, who conversed enthusiastically about the state of art and theatre during the occupation, all the while keeping an eye on the time, as they knew they needed a good night's sleep.

After a first round of drinks, Richard asked Barrault to elaborate on what he had hinted at in the dressing room. "Jean-Louis, you said back at the theatre that you had to assume that the censors who approved your production of *Hamlet* must have had no idea what the play is about. What do you think *Hamlet* is about?"

"Well, that is a huge question, and there are obviously many layers to the play and to its meanings." Here, Barrault lowered his voice so as to be heard only by Richard and Arnaud. "But on the level which should have concerned the censors and the fascist occupiers whom they serve, it is a play about a revolt against the body politic of a corrupt nation, 'Something is rotten in the state of France.' If you want to look at our characters allegorically, why not think of good Queen Gertrude as our beloved French republic, whose rightful lord—our republican form of government—has been treacherously slaughtered and replaced by a counterfeit lord, who wears the uniform and medals of a formerly honored war hero, but who now on a daily basis shamelessly violates the Queen. No wonder then that my Hamlet—while adoring his mother and Queen—treats her cruelly for her acquiescence in betrayal. Hamlet's first victim is Polonius, the conniving co-conspirator who legitimizes the impostor king. The necessary and legitimate regicide is just a matter of time and opportunity. Unfortunately, along the way, there are innocent victims of Hamlet's acts of resistance, Laertes and Ophelia, the two children of the collaborationist Polonius."

Richard, convinced that this was not the time nor place for bold political statements, and beginning to feel uneasy at the direction the conversation had taken, decided to steer Barrault towards safer ground with a naïve question: "But certainly you are also attracted by the play's more universal qualities?"

"Of course. For me, *Hamlet* is first of all a play about the son of a recently murdered father suddenly drawn from his self-indulgent misery by a call to action—and not just any action—a violent and dangerous revenge. He must mature quickly in the few short hours we give him on stage, and accept and assert the new identity thrust upon him. What you saw in the first scene in which Hamlet appears was a whiny, immature, disrespectful, rebellious adolescent, who in subsequent appearances gradually matures in response to the sacred responsibility given to him. In that respect, the play offers some interesting perspective into the role of a male parent. Polonius's semi-comic advice to his son, and his meddlesome interference into his daughter's relationship with Hamlet offer a backdrop onto which we can project our speculation about what might have been the relationship between Hamlet and his father. One possible clue to that relationship is Hamlet's observation that the dead king was lovingly protective of Gertrude, "so loving to my mother that he might not beteem the wind of heaven visit her face too roughly." I willingly assume he would have been equally protective of his child, that is until the time when he must force that child into a terrible adult role. For that purpose he appears before him after death as a terrifying ghost commanding him to commit violence which will ultimately lead to his own death. Hamlet's response to this dramatic change in their relationship and to the dreadful command he receives must reflect the traumatizing and maturing shock he feels in the aftermath of the encounter."

Richard was about to ask another question when Arnaud, who had been keeping a close eye on the time, whispered that it was nearly one a.m., and reminded him that they needed a good night's sleep. Richard excused himself for having to leave, and promised Barrault he would be back in touch about the film project. They graciously thanked their host, who helped them order a cab which took them quickly through nearly deserted streets back to their hotel.

CHAPTER FOUR

"It is suicide to be abroad."

Jacques Friedland heard the German motorcycles long before he could turn and see through the churned up dust the gleaming grey steel of the two bikes and the helmeted uniformed soldiers who motioned him over. There was nowhere to hide, no way to get away, and to run would have been suicide. All he could do was to act surprised that they were interested in him and even more surprised when they searched and handcuffed him, and held him by the side of the road until a silver grey Gestapo Mercedes showed up. Without a word, the police pushed him into the back seat and drove him to the town hall, where he was questioned by an inspector of the Gendarmerie, in the presence of Gustave Rondin, mayor of Apt, and local Gestapo representative Bruno Dietricht.

Rondin had been mayor of Apt for six years before

the Germans arrived, and was clearly not comfortable in his role as mayor of a small "free" village in Vichy France, who was still subject to visits and pressures from the often visible occupiers. He sincerely believed he could do more good for his village and for France by remaining in his position, resisting to the extent possible the occupiers' pressures. He was aware of the Resistance cell operating just outside his village, secretly supporting it. But now he was helpless.

The inspector, after examining Jacques' papers, began the interrogation by politely asking him why he had chosen to live in the isolated village of Roussillon.

"Well, after years of dealing with the difficulties of life in Paris where we own a small art gallery, my wife and I decided in 1937 to move to the south in search of a sunnier climate and a slower pace of life. We maintained ownership of our Paris gallery and asked my wife's cousin to manage it for us, which he has done faithfully. We moved to Vence and opened a second gallery in nearby Saint-Paul, which has a flourishing arts community. The gallery was very successful, and when we sold it four years later, the profit of that sale allowed us to retreat to the peacefulness of this lovely, secluded region. We rent a small apartment in the hotel in Roussillon, where we live in quiet retirement."

"And what are your daily activities?"

"Those of any thoughtful person who has retired to the country. I read, converse with neighbors, play a little pétanque, and walk through the woods where I like to sketch wildlife."

"Are you aware of terrorist activities in the area?"

"Aware? I read about it in the papers, and hear people talk about it."

"Do you know any terrorists?"

"I don't think so. I suppose I might without knowing it. I imagine these are young people with no employment who are desperate for lack of prospects. I heard about the son of a neighbor who ignored the call to forced labor and disappeared into the hills. But I really don't think I know any terrorists."

"What were you doing in Apt this afternoon?"

"Oh, I biked over to compare the availability and price of yarn for my wife. She knits, and the yarn store in Roussillon has very little stock these days, and the prices have risen considerably."

"Where did you go precisely?"

"To Yvette Aigreloup's shop on the rue Mistral. It turns out she has a bit more of a selection and slightly better prices. I plan to come back with my wife tomorrow so she can purchase some, that is if you permit me..."

"Are you a Jew?"

"No. I carry the surname of my father who was a Jewish immigrant from Germany in the early 1890s. But my French Catholic mother had me baptized as an infant, and although I practice little, I consider myself a Catholic. Both my wife and I are counted among the members of the parish in Roussillon."

At this point, Dietricht, who had been listening carefully and taking notes, interrupted the inspector's questions, "Listen, Friedland, we believe that terrorists from the Roussillon area receive and store ammunitions that are parachuted into the area, and that members of this terrorist group were involved in an attack at the Lyon train station during which German soldiers were murdered. What do you know about those activities?"

"Why, nothing at all. I assure you my wife and I strive to live peacefully with our neighbors, and we don't look for trouble."

Dietricht seemed to believe him. The only evidence against Jacques was the suspicions of the woman who owned a florist shop on the rue Mistral in Apt, and she was not believed to be a reliable informer. Jacques certainly did not fit the profile of a terrorist. Convinced that he would get no useful information from this Jewish nature lover, Dietricht ordered Rondin to send him to be interned at Les Milles, with other captured Jews. Minutes later, Jacques was roughly ushered into the back seat of a police vehicle and driven quickly over the dusty dry roads of the Luberon mountain region towards Aix-en-Provence and the camp at Les Milles, where they arrived about an hour later.

As he was being led through the dank hallways of the Les Milles prison complex, the guard was detained by a mild looking gentleman in a clerical collar who asked to be given an opportunity to speak with the prisoner. The guard reluctantly assented. The cleric introduced himself as Father Marie-Benoît, a priest assigned to the camp by the Archbishop of Marseille. He took Jacques aside and asked him why he was being held. Jacques explained that he was suspected of being a member of the Resistance, but that what appeared to be more damaging was his Jewish name. Father Marie-Benoît asked him about his background and if he was baptized, and then smiled and assured him that he would get him released within days after Jacques told him that his two maternal grandparents were both Catholic, that he could provide the name of the parish in Paris where he had been baptized as an infant in 1899, and that he was a parishioner of the church in Roussillon.

Nonetheless, Jacques was relieved of all of his personal belongings, and ushered into a straw-covered foul-smelling cell in which the day's fading light permitted him to distinguish several other men. The one closest to him, a slight, pale young man barely in his twenties, inched over to Jacques to engage him in conversation. "Do you know anything? What will they do to us?" Jacques knew— the Resistance was well aware that the local authorities, in cooperation with the German occupiers, had turned the camp at Les Milles into a way station for the deportation center at Drancy, just outside of Paris. But all he told the young man was that they could be expected to be sent on to Paris.

Father Marie-Benoît was confident he could eventually gain Jacques' release on the basis of a certificate of baptism, and the issuance of a certificate of non-Jewishness, but he also knew that process would take several days or possibly weeks, and that it was unlikely the Germans would keep

Jacques in the camp at Les Milles for more than a day or two. He decided to try to intervene. Early the next morning, he sought out the head of the camp, Eugene Heulin, to appeal to him either to release Jacques immediately or to postpone Jacques' transfer to Paris until his status could be clarified. Heulin listened politely to the priest, then consulted a dossier and glared back at Father Marie-Benoît, "Not only is Friedland a Jew; he has been denounced as a terrorist! I can grant him no special privileges. He will be shipped out to Paris by tomorrow night."

Father Marie-Benoît scrupulously tried to avoid direct contact with the maquis. Any appearance of a chink in his neutrality would immediately result in his being barred from the prison—or worse. He wanted to try to get word to the Roussillon maquis that Jacques was in the prison at Les Milles and about to be sent on to Paris. Aware that he was watched carefully, Father Marie-Benoît knew that he could not call or telegraph to Roussillon. But he was sure he could count on Monsignor du Bois de la Villerabel, archbishop of the Cathedral of Saint-Sauveur in Aix-en-Provence, to help. By noon, he was on a bus into Aix, and by one o'clock he was eating broiled monkfish and parsleyed potatoes with the archbishop in his office in the Cathedral. Over lunch, Father Marie-Benoît explained to the archbishop that he needed his help rather urgently in arranging a meeting with Father Autrand, parish priest in the village of Roussillon. Without seeking to clarify the matter, the archbishop had his secretary send a telegraph to Father Autrand "reminding" him that the archbishop was expecting to meet him that evening at five o'clock with the rest of the regional council at the Abby of Sénanque. Father Marie-Benoît thanked the archbishop, took his leave, and exited the cathedral.

While wondering what was the best way for him to get up to Sénanque to meet with Father Autrand, Father Marie-Benoît lingered for a moment on the terrace of the Gaulois café which runs along the façade of the cathedral, and where several customers were enjoying the coolness of the shade provided by the terrace's chestnut tree and the natural refrigeration emanating from the cathedral's massive wall. While he was standing there lost in thought, a serving woman whom he knew by sight came out, caught his eye and seemed to motion him towards the café's interior.

Father Marie-Benoît entered the café and noticed that there were a couple of customers at the bar discussing grave topics of the day with the bartender. He then glanced into the back room which was nearly empty except for a couple, who looked up from their conversation and motioned for him to come in. He entered and found himself face to face with two senior members of the regional Resistance network, Jean Garcin and Pauline Algoud. Garcin, who was born in 1917 in the village of Vaucluse (now called Fontaine de Vaucluse in honor of its famous landmark), had joined the Resistance in 1940—at a time when there was as yet no real Resistance movement—out of contempt for the anti-republican policies of the Vichy government. He had earned the respect of his Resistance colleagues as a result of his intelligence, resourcefulness, dedication and courage, and was given leadership responsibilities. Now, under the code name Bayard, he was head of special forces for the regional unit. He carried papers which identified him as Jean Rigaud, police inspector from the Lyon commissariat. His companion, Pauline Algoud, was a clever and brave thirty year old Resistance fighter who had been working with Garcin for two years. She was often called upon to disguise herself and deliver messages and occasionally weapons in support of prisoner escapes. Father Marie-Benoît had known Garcin for years, and was well aware of his activities which he admired and respected.

"Father, you seemed lost in thought."

"I am, and perhaps you can help. It is about the arrest of Jacques Friedland."

"Is he interned at Les Milles?"

"Yes, he is." Father Marie-Benoît told Garcin and Algoud all that he knew, including the details of his conversations with Jacques, the camp commandant Eugene Heulin, and the archbishop.

Garcin listened intently. "I am glad we ran into you. We are here on other business, but I have heard of Friedland's arrest, and we want to help. You have done well to bring us this information, but now you should get back to the prison. It is too dangerous for you to be further involved in this. Pauline will travel up to Sénanque to see Father Autrand, and then on to Roussillon."

The grateful and relieved priest left to return to Les Milles, while Garcin quickly outlined instructions for Pauline to take to the Roussillon maquis.

"They are going to want to rescue him, and I understand. We need some good news. Make sure they realize that to undertake anything in the prison is impossible, but there may be some possibility of escape from the train going north. Tell them they have my approval, and that we will alert the Gap maquis to be prepared to offer support. I suggest you drive up to Sénanque, meet Father Autrand there and take him with you up to Roussillon. After you confer with the Roussillon maquis about their plans, see what you can find out about who denounced Friedland, and then look for me back here tomorrow afternoon around four o'clock at the Deux Frères café."

Father Autrand of the Roussillon parish was surprised and flattered to receive a telegram from the archbishop, and a little embarrassed that he did not really remember having known about this council meeting before. He was even more surprised when he arrived by bus at the Abby and found, not the archbishop, but a young woman in a nun's uniform; it was Pauline Algoud who introduced herself as a member of the Resistance's social services network. She explained to Father Autrand what had been learned from Father Marie-Benoît about the imprisonment of Jacques Friedland and asked for his help in bringing it to the attention of the Roussillon maquis. Father Autrand was a meek man, but of great integrity. He accepted the challenge, and, while returning to Roussillon with Pauline Algoud, found a way to get word to the commander of the Roussillon maquis, Félix Arnaud, of Jacques Friedland's imprisonment at Les Milles, by leaving a message with the owner of the Resistance friendly hardware store at the entrance to the village.

Within hours, word had spread among members of the Roussillon cell, and Arnaud called an emergency meeting for that night. At midnight, eleven men and women were seated in a small barn just outside the village on benches around a central table, lit by kerosene lanterns. The windows had been boarded over so that the light would not attract attention.

Present at the meeting on that night of June 8, in addition to Arnaud, were Samuel Beckett, Richard Rosendale, Joanne Friedland, Gaston Jouvaud, who owned the village hardware store and who had delivered Father Autrand's message to Arnaud, Martin and Catherine Aubenas, who owned a farm on the edge of the town, and who were also supported by their sons' work in the ochre mines, Charles Pouget, who had left the village to work in a factory in Lyon but then returned to support the Vaucluse Resistance, Antoine Biron, the village butcher, Léon Favre, a foreman in the mines, and Pauline Algoud.

Catherine Aubenas had been in Apt late that afternoon and had first become aware of Jacques' denunciation and eventual arrest. She told her story after Arnaud asked her to tell the group what she knew.

"It was that awful Minteux woman, who runs the florist shop on the rue Mistral, the woman from Paris. She was talking in the doorway of the shop with the German who had come through on patrol, just at the moment when Jacques rode past the store. She took the German inside and apparently told him what she knew and what she suspected about Jacques. He radioed ahead to a motorcycle unit which intercepted him outside the village. Françoise Rigano told me later that she saw him taken into the Town Hall in handcuffs."

At this point, Pauline Algoud asked pointedly if Catherine were absolutely sure that Minteux had been the one who had denounced Jacques.

"Absolutely. She was seen by several people talking with the German police. Besides she has a photo of Pétain in her shop, and it is common knowledge that she gives special deals and who knows what else to the Germans."

Arnaud told his colleagues that Jacques had been imprisoned at Les Milles, without giving any indication of the source of his information. He had absolute faith in his maquis brethren, but knew better than to burden them with information potentially fatal to three good priests. After pausing for a few minutes, deep in thought, he added, "We have some sources that will help us get information from Les Milles. I know that you all love and respect Jacques, and want to help him. We must keep uppermost in our minds the overall cause that we along with Jacques have been fighting for, and avoid any rash actions that will imperil other members of our unit. On the other hand, Jacques' capture provides us with an impetus to move forward with plans already under discussion to disrupt the Germans' prisoner transport network from the south of France to Paris and on to Germany and Poland."

The action forces of the Resistance had by the spring of 1943 established operational priorities as well as strict protocols to reduce betrayals and arrests. Their primary objective was to interfere with the German occupiers through the destruction and theft of their military supplies, and the interruption of communication and transportation networks. They also sought to lay the groundwork for a general insurrection to coincide with the anticipated invasion of allied forces. An overriding concern of the Resistance, in the face of aggressive anti-terrorist campaigns by the French and German police and a demoralizing wave of denunciations by *pétainiste* collaborators, was the protection of loyal citizens from betrayal and arrest, and the liberation of arrested Resistance fighters.

The Resistance movement had been heavily damaged in April of 1943 by the arrest and subsequent betrayal of one of its members, Jean Multon, in Marseille. Multon had been second in command of the regional Combat section of the Resistance network, and, following his arrest, had revealed information ultimately fatal to more than one hundred Resistance fighters throughout the region. This recent tragedy weighed heavily in Arnaud's decision to give high priority to freeing Jacques Friedland, and in Jean Garcin's approval and support of the mission. The Resistance network needed a victory.

The next morning, Pauline Algoud, who had spent the night at the Hotel de la Poste in Roussillon, set off for the Fleurs de Nice flower shop in Apt, managed by Adèle Minteux. She found the store on the rue Mistral, wandered in, and looked at the arrangements in the front of the store for awhile, pretending to try to make up her mind.

As she glanced around the tidy shop her eyes stopped at the framed portrait of a uniformed Philippe Pétain behind the counter long enough for the shopkeeper to notice, walk over to her and comment, "He is really our only hope."

Pauline tried to sound approving. "I am afraid you are right."

That was all Mme Minteux needed. "Certainly he is very old, and people say he may be losing his grip, but he stepped forward in a time of crisis, saved the country, and continues to maintain order in the face of the threats that surround us."

Pauline felt Mme Minteux needed a little encouragement. "The threats?"

"From the Jews, communists, and anarchists who would destroy the country for their own gain!"

"Of course."

Mme Minteux, fully launched now, continued her tirade. "They are all around us. We see Jews who don't work, don't serve the country, who seem to have all the money they need, and who manipulate the black market to satisfy their greed. They plot with the communists and anarchists who would sell us all to the Russians. We got one of them arrested just yesterday. Did you know that within three kilometers of Apt, there is a landing field where they parachute in guns and explosives to arm the terrorists?"

Pauline, alarmed by this last statement, assumed a conspiratorial air. "If this is true, Madame, and you are aware of the location of this landing field, you need to alert the police. I have a friend, Inspector Rigaud of the Gendarmerie, whose mission is to track terrorists in the region. May I send him to you?"

"Of course. I can lead him to the place!"

"I will have him visit you today, or tomorrow at the latest. In the meantime I urge you to be careful, and not talk about your information to anyone. Are there many people aware of this landing site?"

"Oh my, of course! They probably have spies everywhere! No, I don't think so. And it is really just a suspicion that my husband and I have, because we saw cars leaving there late one night."

"I see. I will encourage Inspector Rigaud to look into this. It sounds very important! Oh, I almost forgot, I would like this bouquet please. For my mother's birthday."

"Certainly. That will be eighteen francs, please. And thank you!"

* * * * * * * *

The following afternoon, Jean Garcin and Alphonse Begou strode into the Fleurs de Nice floral shop on the rue Mistral in Apt. Begou was a thirty-five year old tradesman from the village of Le Thor whom Garcin had recruited into the Resistance. Garcin presented Mme Minteux his card identifying him as Inspector Jean Rigaud of the Lyon commissariat, and introduced Begou as his lieutenant. As there was no one else in the shop, he wasted no time and went right to the point of his visit.

"Mme Minteux, I know that you have already been very helpful to our anti-terrorist effort by denouncing a traitor. And I understand that you have additional information about a possible parachute landing site in the hills around Apt. We have long suspected that the terrorists are armed through parachute drops somewhere in this region, so any information you can give us may be crucial."

"As I told the young woman yesterday, my husband and I are not absolutely sure. That is why

I never mentioned it before. But one night about ten days ago, as we were returning home from Bonnieux through back roads, we passed a group of cars and small trucks stopped on the edge of a field, and we saw some men loading crates into the back of one of the trucks."

"That does indeed sound suspicious. Can you take us there?"

"Certainly. We can lead you out there right after I close the shop at seven this evening. I will need my husband to join us, as he knows the roads better than I do. Is that OK?"

"Of course. By all means, bring your husband along. We will come by here at seven this evening. In the meantime, talk to no one about this. Thank you, Mme Minteux."

Chapter Five

*"Let this vile dust fall back
upon the viler worms."*

After a few hours of sleep, Olivier d'Anglade was back in his Paris office at seven a.m. to begin to put together the information that had started to come in about the prison train leaving Drancy the following day. As he sifted through the coded messages, he sensed some uncertainty about the precise route. The Germans had carefully muddied the trail, preparing alternate routes, and setting up decoy trains, specifically to thwart any Resistance attacks. D'Anglade decided that through a couple of official visits, one to Louis Darquier de Pellepoix, the Vichy government's Commissioner for Jewish Questions (CGQJ), and one to the newly appointed Drancy prison commandant, Alois Brunner, he might be able to shake loose some additional useful details.

At nine a.m., he appeared at the CGQJ Paris headquarters in his chauffeured government car, and demanded to see Commissioner Darquier, who received him in his office thirty minutes later. In May 1942, Louis Darquier had replaced Xavier Vallat as Commissioner of Jewish Affairs. In that role he was head of a vast bureaucracy which oversaw the administration of laws restricting the rights of Jews in France, and which had specific responsibility for the transfer of Jewish prisoners from the Gendarmerie to the Gestapo. While Darquier's predecessor, Xavier Vallat, had brought to the position a measure of legal and ethical concerns within the framework of the strict anti-Semitic laws decreed by the Vichy government, Darquier was an unscrupulous zealot, a right wing adventurer and thug who profited from the misery he caused others. Darquier was born in 1897 in Cahors, the son of a doctor. He fought bravely as a soldier in World War I, but abandoned his unit before he was officially discharged. He worked for businesses in France and Holland before a short stint as a ranch hand in Australia. Back in Paris in February 1934, he was slightly wounded in a confrontation between his right wing Action Française colleagues and police at the Place de la

Concorde. He created an organization of those wounded during that event, and declared himself its president. With that as a platform, he was elected to the Paris Municipal Council, where in 1938 he distinguished himself with a virulent anti-Semitic speech in which he blamed Jews among other things for starting and losing World War I for France. He used his rabid anti-Semitism as a leverage to secure funding from unofficial German government sources, with which he founded a weekly anti-Semitic journal, *La France Enchaînée*. During the first two years of the occupation, he involved himself actively in anti-Jewish propaganda, often supported by German funds. In 1942, the Germans urged his appointment to the CGQJ to replace Xavier Vallat.

Darquier's reign as commissioner was marked by mean spirited anti-Jewish propaganda, unparalleled cooperation with the Gestapo, an enthusiastic surrender to the German's final solution, and disastrous administrative practices. Within the commission, officials were hired and fired on the basis of proven anti-Semitic zeal and cronyism. Darquier chose as his private secretary Pierre Gallien, owner of a tire-recapping business in the Paris suburb of Neuilly, who had helped finance some of Darquier's ventures, and was co-editor with him of *La France Enchaînée.* Darquier and Gallien had been arrested together in 1939 for beating up the distributor of a journal sympathetic to Jews. Eventually the two fell out, which resulted in a fist fight in the CGQJ offices and Gallien's dismissal.

One of Darquier's most ludicrous acts was to appoint in November 1942 Henri Labroue, an anti-Semitic zealot, to a newly created chair at the Sorbonne in the History of Judaism. Labroue was a history professor from Bordeaux who had been elected to the national Chamber of Deputies as a representative of a right wing political party. His propagandistic, anti-Jewish lectures were attended by only a handful of regular students, reinforced by a number of hecklers who were routinely photographed for identification by the CGQJ.

A December 20, 1943, memo from the German occupying administration to the Vichy government included Darquier on a list of officials whose resignation was required by the German government. An internal memo from the head of propaganda sources of the German embassy in Paris had earlier cited a unanimous opinion among German officials that Darquier was "absolutely useless in everything."

D'Anglade had had frequent dealings with

Commissioner Darquier. He had nothing but contempt for his values, his incompetence, his opportunism, and his mean-spiritedness, but he had learned that by feigned cordiality and camaraderie he could manipulate Darquier and gain useful information. And so d'Anglade smiled as he entered Darquier's lavish office.

"Good morning, Baron! To what do I owe the honor of this early morning visit?"

"Good morning, Commissioner. I understand that you are preparing to deport a large number of French citizens in the coming days to prison camps outside of France."

"Yes, Baron. Technically French citizens I suppose still, but almost all Jews. Our police forces have been extremely efficient in achieving the goal of delivering 10,000 Jews from the unoccupied zone for deportation. Thanks to their dedication, the prison facilities here are overextended, and so we will be deporting a couple of thousand this week. The train leaves late tomorrow afternoon. I will be happy to invite you personally to observe the entire process: the assignment of prisoners to train cars, their proper treatment, and the orderly departure."

"Thank you, Commissioner, that will not be necessary. I count on the Gendarmerie to respect the rights of the prisoners, as well as international protocol. I won't attend personally. I may send a senior staff member, just to be able to reassure friends and foes that our monitoring of prisoner transfers is serious. Could you give me a laissez-passer for tomorrow in the name of Raymond Crosatier?"

"Certainly, Baron. With my personal stamp on it, M. Crosatier can come and go as he pleases."

"Thank you, Commissioner."

"There is, Baron, a larger issue which I would like to discus with you."

"Certainly. What is that, Commissioner?"

"It seems to me that you who are so forceful in your determination that the letter of the law be respected in our dealings with prisoners have nonetheless allowed certain of our anti-Jewish laws to be flouted within your own ministry circles."

D'Anglade continued smiling impassively, while reviewing quickly in his mind whether he might have been personally careless in a way that would have come to Darquier's attention and thereby left himself open to suspicion. "What are you referring to, M. Darquier?"

"It is obvious that advance warnings of some police raids have permitted Jews to flee in time and escape our dragnet. This has occurred recently in Paris and in the unoccupied zone. The Prefect of the Bouches du Rhône reports that his services have interrupted radio warnings from London specifically alerting Jews to raids, whose exact timing would have been known only within the higher circles of the Interior Ministry!"

D'Anglade relaxed a bit, knowing that those warnings could in no circumstance be traced to himself or to others close to him. He sighed with feigned sympathy, "Such betrayals are certainly a breach of professional responsibility."

"And they seriously interfere with our work. In the Ardèche Department, in a raid last month, police were able to arrest only 137 of the Jews on their list. In Haute Savoie, they arrested only 42 of 91!"

"And yet, Commissioner, you have just assured me that our prisons are overflowing, and that we are on target to meet the occupiers' quotas."

"Perhaps, but then there is the treacherous example of General Robert de Saint-Vincent, commander of the military for the region of Lyon, who refused to allow his soldiers to assist in the deportation of Jews from that city!"

"I remind you that he was relieved of his post

within forty-eight hours, Commissioner. But tell me, do you have specific information, or even suspicions, regarding Ministry of the Interior officials who may be betraying the government?"

"I have vague suspicions, but no specific information, Baron. It is public knowledge that certain prefects lack the needed enthusiasm for our cause. Prefect François Martin of the Tarn and Garonne Department for example seems to sympathize with the enemies of deportation."

D'Anglade nodded. He had no interest in pursuing this conversation, reassured that Darquier's irritation was not based on any suspicions pointed towards him or his associates. "I assure you that I have discussed these issues with President Laval, and that he shares your dismay."

"Do you, Baron?"

"To some extent, but I try not to let the private opinions of my ministry colleagues interfere with my appreciation of their loyalty, their respect for the law, their competence in administering it, and their ultimate usefulness to our nation."

"And in that, Baron, we disagree profoundly."

"Perhaps. I do thank you for your courtesy in receiving me, Commissioner, and for the pass for my associate, M. Crosatier."

D'Anglade sped away in his chauffeured car, clutching the valuable prison pass which Darquier had given to him on the way out, and headed out of Paris towards Drancy. There was little mid-morning traffic on this overcast Friday morning in early June. As his car sped along the Avenue Jean Jaurès towards the Porte de Pantin, d'Anglade found the boulevard dark, dreary and sinister, with few pedestrians and many of the soot blackened store fronts boarded up. The suburban towns of Pantin and Bobigny seemed a bit more animated, but piles of curbside garbage lined their streets awaiting the increasingly unpredictable waste removal service, and the grimy façades of the stores and businesses along Departmental Route 115 which passed through those towns and into Drancy seemed to fade into the heavy cloud cover.

Just after eleven a.m., the car arrived at the gate of the prison, and d'Anglade asked politely to see the prison commandant Alois Brunner, who received him in his office almost immediately. Brunner was one of the Reich's most influential bureaucrats, Adolph Eichmann's trusted lieutenant in the implementation of the Reich's "final solution." His fanatic dedication to racial purity and his cruelty in the practical details of carrying out

Reich policy were well known. Stories of his excesses circulated after the war amidst astonishment that he escaped prosecution and was allowed to live out his life in Syria.

Until the arrival of Brunner, the prison commandants had been French appointees of the Gendarmerie. But the Germans chafed at what they considered French bureaucratic incompetence. Ironically, they were outraged at the reports of inhumane treatment, filthy living conditions, and inadequate nourishment of prisoners at Drancy; and when the departure of a deportation train had been delayed in the fall of 1942, Adolph Eichmann had personally called Heinz Röthke, head of the Jewish office within the German police hierarchy in Paris, to express his outrage and to demand a change in prison administration. Following the transfer of prison administration to the Germans in the late spring of 1943, there were no more train delays, and the housing and food arrangements actually improved for prisoners of the camp under Brunner's administration.

D'Anglade had not yet met Brunner, who had assumed his new post just the week before. He had received reports that the man seemed to have no personality, no interests, no passions, beyond his stupid dedication to sending innocent victims to extermination camps. D'Anglade nonetheless smiled and extended his hand as he entered Brunner's Spartan office within the prison complex's crowded administrative wing. Brunner spoke excellent French.

"Good morning, Baron! Thank you for coming to visit. I have been eager to meet you."

"Good morning, Commandant. I thought we should meet, since, as I believe you have been informed, I am charged by our government with the legal monitoring of the transfer of prisoners from the Gendarmerie to the Gestapo."

"Of course, Baron d'Anglade. I am aware of your responsibilities, and also with your reputation as a man of great legal stature, unquestioned loyalty and integrity. I think you should be pleased with some of the changes we have made in prison administration to eliminate the appalling inadequacies uncovered by our police in the treatment of prisoners."

"Yes, and I thank you for that, as I understand that housing conditions have improved, and that prisoners now have a healthier and more varied diet."

"That all seems so obvious. It is not difficult to

keep prison cells clean and sanitized. If the prisoners are to be useful additions to our work camps in the east, they must be healthy and reasonably nourished! And both of our countries and the prisoners themselves are best served by an orderly, efficient and predictable imprisonment and deportation process."

"Certainly. I will be sending an observer tomorrow to monitor the transfer of prisoners for the deportation train leaving in the afternoon."

"Of course. Your observer will find the process orderly and efficient."

D'Anglade steered the conversation for several minutes towards clearing up some murky technical and legal issues affecting the transfer of prisoners, before off-handedly asking, "If you don't mind my asking, where in Germany will you be sending these particular deportees?"

A cloud seemed to darken for a fraction of a second Brunner's bright blue eyes. He stared hard at d'Anglade before answering with all of his former conviviality.

"Actually, they are being sent to Poland, to camps near Auschwitz. But once they have passed the border at Mulhouse, their ultimate destination should be of no concern to the French government."

"No, of course not. Would you prefer that I not inform the Minister of the ultimate destination? I can keep that information confidential."

"Perhaps, Baron. Thank you. His ability to deny that knowledge may be useful to all of us. Is there anything else I can do for you?"

"No. I appreciate your candor and courtesy."

"I think we can have, Baron d'Anglade, a good mutual understanding. Your aristocratic lineage makes you a natural patriot, and I appreciate that. I wish you a good day."

Olivier sped away in his chauffeured car, savoring the useful knowledge that the train would pass the French border at Mulhouse, but also revolted by his own obsequiousness in the face of evil.

* * * * * * * *

Emboldened by his first successes at passing in and out of the Drancy prison dressed as a gendarme, Arnaud's first thought upon awakening that morning was to get back into the prison to pass on to Beckett the good news that the escape attempt had the approval of the Paris Resistance, and that they would furnish additional useful information in the next several hours.

He changed into the uniform again in the train station bathroom, and walked briskly through the prison gate flashing an official looking ID before anyone even thought to challenge his identity. He walked purposefully in the direction of the cell where he knew Friedland and Beckett were being held, but veered off down another hallway, when he saw a prison guard standing in the doorway of that cell. He watched from twenty-five meters down the hall, as the guard escorted Beckett out of the cell and in the direction away from where Arnaud stood observing them. Alert to the danger of the situation, he followed the guard and Beckett discreetly towards the administrative wing, where the guard delivered Beckett into a small private office.

* * * * * * * *

Beckett and Friedland lay quietly on the floor of their still dark cell. They resisted efforts by other prisoners to engage them in conversation, and resisted also the temptation to talk together, fearing that might draw unwanted attention. Beckett was preoccupied by the certainty that the prison administration would quickly realize that there was no paperwork explaining his presence in the prison.

He had during the night transferred his pistol, and a small collection of tools sewn into his uniform to Jacques, in case he was subjected to interrogation and a search.

A bit later in the morning, a guard opened the door of the cell, and motioned for him to get up. Without a glance at Jacques who was staring worriedly at him, Beckett rose and followed the gendarme. He was led into a small office, where the guard searched him and handcuffed his wrists to each arm of the chair in which he was placed before withdrawing.

A German in civilian clothes entered the room and sat opposite him. He questioned him in English.

"Mr. Beckett, where did you acquire your false passport?"

"It is not a false passport."

"Come on, now. We know you are Samuel Beckett, an Irish writer of poor reputation, and yet you have a passport in the name of Milo O'Shea."

"It is perfectly acceptable for a writer to adopt a pseudonym. That is what I have done. I applied for and was granted an official Irish passport in the name of O'Shea, a pseudonym I adopted two year ago."

"Why are you in France?"

"Because I have more loyalty to France than to my home country."

"How do you support yourself?"

"As a day laborer in an agricultural community."

"Why?"

"To have enough money to live on while I write."

"Are you engaged in terrorist activities?"

"No."

"Do you know others who are?"

"No."

"Do you know why were you arrested?"

"No, can you tell me?"

"Yes, I can. Despite your pseudonym, our police have succeeded in identifying you as an enemy of the state, the subversive and deviant writer Samuel Beckett."

"Subversive? Deviant?"

"Do you deny that you are the author of *Murphy*, a novel about a sexual pervert with anti-social tendencies, in which you exalt a lifestyle which subverts youth and promotes homosexuality?"

"There is nothing exalting about my novel, I assure you. I guess I have to admit that the lifestyle of my novel's hero is a poor example to youth. Do you imprison people for that?"

"We do."

Beckett was actually intrigued and relieved by the direction the interrogation had taken. He certainly hadn't wanted to be released. He was amazed the Gestapo seemed to know so much about him: had they actually read *Murphy*? What a fortunate turn of events that its publication constituted a crime that would keep him in prison. His interrogator went on, "The Reich's goal of moral purity is menaced by writers like you, whose obvious talent is channeled antisocially. Your arrest warrant from 1940 makes that abundantly clear."

At this, Beckett had to restrain a gasp. "What a joke!" he thought. He knew there was no 1940 arrest warrant for *Murphy*. But the more he thought about it, the more he marveled. Who could have created that little fiction, and all in the last twenty-four hours?

"You will be deported with the other social misfits, perverts and Jews. The guard will take you back to your cell."

The guard entered, and Beckett was only slightly surprised to see it was Félix Arnaud, once again in a French police uniform. Arnaud uncuffed him, searched him again roughly, and lead him back to his cell, without a word. As he settled back onto the floor of his cell, Sam reached into his left pants pocket where it seemed Arnaud's hand had lingered, and pulled out discreetly a folded piece of paper.

CHAPTER SIX

"Are you going in my direction?"

After the fall of Paris, and the French-German Armistice of 1940, Richard Rosendale, his wife Martine Lenouet, and Jacques and Joanne Friedland were at first comfortable in the thought that they could wait out the war in the Hotel Miramar which Richard and Martine owned and managed in Vence, ten miles north of Nice. However, the arrests in April and May, 1941, of hundreds of Jews in Marseille, Nice and Cannes sent a ripple of fear through their happy establishment.

Although baptized as a child in 1899, Jacques Friedland was the son of German Jewish painter Isaac Friedland and his French Catholic wife Anne-Marie, who had settled in Paris in the 1890s. Jacques had inherited his father's aesthetic wisdom and his mother's business sense. His and

Joanne's Friedland Gallery, established in 1927 in the rue de Seine in Paris, had been successful enough to allow them in 1937 to open a second gallery in Saint-Paul de Vence, which they managed directly while leaving the Paris gallery under the care of Joanne's cousin, Alfred Pons.

Following the events of April and May of 1941, Jacques and Joanne came to realize that his background and their name represented a danger, living where they lived, only ten miles from Nice. The staff of Marshal Pétain having noted with dismay the large number of Jewish refugees who had sought refuge in the area around Nice, Prefect Marcel Ribière of the Alpes-Maritime Department responded with a massive operation which was orchestrated by Henri Chavin, secretary-general for the national police, and which resulted in the arrest of several hundred Jews between April 25 and May 3, 1941. The Prefect justified the arrests of foreign Jews with unfounded accusations of anti-government and black market activities. Some of those arrested were assigned to internment camps; others were ordered to leave the area.

Dismayed by these events, the Friedlands decided in the summer of 1941 to leave the area. They sold their gallery in Saint-Paul to a Spanish buyer, Roberto Otero, at a reasonable profit. Through friends in the art world, they had learned of the isolated village of Roussillon, thirty-five miles from Avignon, which seemed to be relatively safe from German intervention, and decided to move there and live on the income from their sale of the Saint-Paul gallery, and money sent by Alfred Pons who continued to manage their gallery in Paris.

The Friedlands' decision, though painful and desperate, was far easier to make than Richard's and Martine's. They faced no imminent danger. As an American, Richard felt no particular threat. The hotel they had opened in 1938 continued to flourish in 1941, a happy haven from the harsh realities of cities in the free zone, and the even harsher realities of occupied France. Their rooms were always full, and the hotel dining room attracted people from throughout the region.

But the misery of their friends in Paris, and the imminent danger threatening the Friedlands made their lives every day more distressing. They became aware of people in the village actively working in the developing Resistance network and involved in clandestine operations to arm and provide information to groups of *maquisards* operating from the caves and isolated basements of houses spread throughout the lower Alps region. Richard and Martine ultimately decided to commit themselves totally to the Resistance cause, and to leave behind their comfortable life as hotel owners. After much thought and anguish, in late summer 1941, they accepted an offer and sold the hotel in Vence to Daniel Varlet. With the profit of that sale, they were able to purchase the Hôtel de la Poste in Roussillon, and had enough left over to supplement the meager income their new hotel might generate. They moved to Roussillon in the fall of 1941, along with the Friedlands.

Although small and isolated, the village of Roussillon provided an active political base to support the growing underground Resistance movement in the area. The village council had long been dominated by socialists and communists, whose strong popular support was a reflection of the economic hard times that had plagued the village in the twentieth century. The commercialization in the 1930s of the ochre pigments mined from the cliffs surrounding the village had provided only temporary relief from the long term decline brought about by the disappearance of the active silkworm industry, which had prospered early in the century. By the

1940s, the ochre industry was in serious decline, and no one imagined the prosperity that tourism would bring to the village and the region in the second half of the twentieth century. Life was hard for the villagers during the war years, and many eagerly backed the Resistance.

On October 6, 1941, when the Friedlands and Rosendales went to the Town Hall in Roussillon to register their arrival, they noticed on the registry the name of Samuel B. Beckett, of Ireland, who, along with his French companion, Suzanne Dumesnil, had recently moved into the village.

Born in Dublin in 1906, Samuel Beckett had enjoyed a materially comfortable childhood. His father William, who had built the family house in the Foxrock suburb of Dublin, was a surveyor and his mother a nurse. A natural athlete, Beckett excelled at tennis and cricket. He studied French, Italian, and English at Trinity College, Dublin, from 1923 to 1927, then taught at Campbell College in Belfast, and was later named lecteur d'anglais at the École Normale Supérieure in Paris. While there, he met fellow Irish author James Joyce, and worked as Joyce's assistant. He enjoyed a close relationship with the Joyce family, until Beckett's unhappy relationship with Joyce's daughter Lucia caused their friendship to cool. In 1930, Beckett returned to Trinity College as a lecturer but resigned that position at the end of 1931, and began several years of travel in Europe, especially in Germany. He returned to Ireland in 1937 and published his first novel, *Murphy*, in 1938. His French translation of *Murphy* was published in 1939. In Paris, in January 1938, Beckett was stabbed in the chest and nearly killed, an incident which led to his relationship with Suzanne Dechevaux-Dumesnil, who had visited him in his hospital room.

At the time of the German occupation, Beckett left Paris, seeking refuge with friends in Arcachon. After a few months there, he returned to Paris in the fall of 1940 and joined a Resistance cell. His work consisted of translating, organizing, and delivering documents. In the summer of 1941, their cell was compromised, and Suzanne and Beckett fled their apartment, just ahead of the Gestapo. For a few weeks they took refuge in the home of writer Nathalie Sarraute just outside of Paris, until they were able to secure passage into the unoccupied zone and eventually to the village of Roussillon, where they survived partly on his family income, and through his work on the Borelly farm, and Suzanne's music lessons. They lived in a rented windmill on the outskirts of the village but often took meals at the Hôtel de la Poste.

An unlikely set of personal experiences and dramatic world events had conspired to bring together in the then fairly anonymous village of Roussillon in the Luberon Mountains these six characters: Richard Rosendale, an American sculptor and painter, his wife Martine Lenouet, a hotelkeeper, Samuel Beckett, an Irish writer, his companion Suzanne Dumesnil, a music teacher, and Jacques and Joanne Friedland, retired Parisian gallery owners. They had bonded as a result of common interests in the worlds of the arts and ideas, through the extraordinary circumstances that brought them together, and through their common efforts to support the Resistance army operating in the mountains around Roussillon.

The leader of the maquis forces in the Luberon Mountain region was Félix Arnaud, a young veteran of the Spanish Civil War. Arnaud was a handsome and athletically built man of thirty-two. He was considered brilliant, fearless and deeply committed to the anti-fascist cause. Few members of the local maquis knew his personal history.

Félix Arnaud was the only son of Alicia Rovira Arnaud and Gustave Arnaud. His mother Alicia was one of the three adult survivors of the Mexican occupation of Clipperton Island, a small atoll 600 miles off the Mexican coast. Arnaud had moved to Nice with his widowed mother as a seven year old child in 1917. While he had only vague and confused memories of the first six years of his life on Clipperton, his mother Alicia had frequently encouraged him to peruse the documents and pictures she kept in a small chest in her bedroom, documents of their life on Clipperton, including a clear photograph of her, Alicia, and the other two surviving women posing on the beach in front of their wooden cabins. In the photo, his mother looks boldly but sadly towards the camera, her gentle features relaxed but unsmiling, wearing a neat white collarless blouse. The other two women, Altagracia Quiroz and Tirza Randon, seem to be talking to each other, Altagracia smiling warmly. The most revealing documents in the chest were the court records and newspaper accounts of the three women's trial in California for the murder of the lighthouse guard Victoriano Alvarez. Arnaud found the story they told chilling but ultimately reassuring.

In September 1905, Captain Gustave Arnaud, Félix's father, arrived on Clipperton Island as governor, with eleven soldiers and 60 Italian workers to exploit the island's guano mines. Harsh living conditions and dwindling resources gradually reduced the island's population, with the result that by 1914, there were only about thirty of the settlers still remaining. Mexican authorities urged the remaining colonists to return to Mexico, but Captain Arnaud declined the offer. Their numbers were further reduced by disease in the following year. On June 26, 1915, Captain Arnaud, thinking he had spotted a sinking ship off the coast, led several of the remaining men out to sea in a small boat. The boat capsized and all of the men were devoured by sharks before the horrified eyes of the women, and the remaining adult male on the island, Victoriano Alvarez. Alvarez immediately declared himself king of the island and subjected the three women to his will. At the end of a year, the three women conspired to murder Alvarez. Tirza Randon induced him to drink a large quantity of the rice beer produced on the island, and while he was sleeping off the effects, the three women attacked him with hammers. The same day, an American Navy ship patrolling in the area landed on Clipperton, discovered the survivors and the corpse of Alvarez, and took them all back to California.

The Ochre Cliffs of Roussillon

The Village of Roussillon

The Prison Camp at Les Milles

The Prison Camp at Les Milles

The Gaulois Café in Aix-en-Provence

The Rue Mistral in Apt

The Minteux Flower Shop

The Drancy Transit Camp

After a brief trial, an American jury acquitted the three women. Altagracia Quiroz and Tirza Randon returned to Mexico, but Alicia Arnaud decided to accept the invitation of her dead husband's parents to join them in Nice.

Philippe and Monique Arnaud had warmly welcomed the young widow and her child. Their comfortable status—he had made a small fortune in the newly created refrigeration industry in southern France—permitted Félix to adjust rapidly to life in France with the help of private tutors. Bright and alert, he rapidly mastered French and German, while maintaining his fluency in both Spanish and English. He was admitted to the lycée Jules Ferry in Nice in 1928, brilliantly passed his baccalauréat in 1932, and enrolled in the University to study political science. Well on his way towards completing the *aggrégation* in 1936, he abandoned his studies to fight in the Spanish Civil War with his Communist colleagues. He returned to Nice in 1938, and joined the Resistance in 1940.

Although the French-German armistice of 1940 had created an unoccupied zone in the south of France which remained free of German troops until late in 1942, many patriotic French men and women had repudiated the Vichy Government of

Marshall Philippe Pétain almost immediately following the National Assembly's vote of July 10, 1940, yielding all authority to Pétain, committing themselves to resisting this affront to their traditions of republicanism. Subsequent legislative decisions and executive orders reinforced their resolve, as the Pétain government became increasingly fascistic. Although the numbers of those opposed to the policies of the Vichy government continued to grow throughout the war years, public displays of opposition were infrequent and short-lived. On July 14, 1942, anti-Vichy activists mounted a large public demonstration in Avignon, the capital of the Vaucluse department. The Resistance radio network, Radio de la France Libre, had urged opponents of the Vichy government to rally in all the cities of France. Thousands gathered in front of the Avignon train station and marched to the city hall. The crowd included members of the local Resistance networks but also merchants, doctors and lawyers. Assembled in front of the town hall, they spontaneously began singing the Marseillaise, until armed police arrived and broke up the peaceful demonstration.

Private expressions of opposition were even more

dangerous. Pétain personally approved the creation of a political police force, a militia, under the direction of Joseph Darnand, which patrolled cities and villages and had the authority to arrest, try and summarily execute suspected terrorists. Denunciations were common.

Nonetheless, by the spring of 1943, the ranks of the Resistance fighters in the Vaucluse region had swelled. Patriots embraced the republican ideals of the Resistance, increasingly angry and revolted by Vichy policies, specifically disturbed by legislation limiting the rights of Jews and by large scale arrests of them, the German invasion of the south in November 1942, which resulted in a repressive German military and police presence, and most recently the February 1943 law which imposed deportation for forced labor in Germany on all men over the age of twenty.

The hilly region between Roussillon and Apt was of strategic importance to the Resistance movement. Weapons and other needed supplies were routinely parachuted into southern France by the allied armies in England and North Africa. Ideal parachute landing sites had to be remote and hidden from view, but still accessible by roads and close enough to stockpiling centers so that weapons and explosives could be quickly transported and hidden. The terrain between Roussillon and Apt, between the Luberon mountain range to the south, and the lower Alps to the north, met those strategic geographic needs. In the course of the war, more than 200 parachute drops were made into the region: sten automatic rifles, machine guns, traditional weapons, plastic explosives, and sacks filled with currency literally fell from the sky and were quickly gathered up by waiting Resistance fighters. Occasionally soldiers were also dropped onto the sites, including one very famous one.

On December 31, 1941, Jean Moulin, an agent of General Charles de Gaulle who in London had organized the Free France government in exile, parachuted into the region with the assignment to unite the Resistance network. Until this time, Resistance units operated independently and occasionally at cross-purposes. By November 1942, Moulin had succeeded in creating the United Resistance Movements which brought together the three major Resistance organizations, Combat, Libération and Franc-Tireur.

The director of parachute operations for the region, one of the most colorful members of the Vaucluse maquis, had his headquarters in the remote village of Céreste outside of Apt. He was known to his Resistance colleagues as Captain Alexandre, the nom de guerre of surrealist poet René Char. Char, who was born in 1888 in the Vaucluse city of Île sur la Sorgue, was the son of the mayor of that city, Joseph Char. Char was tall and athletic and a fanatic rugby player. But he was also a lover of French poetry—especially Villon, Racine, Vigny, Nerval, and Baudelaire—whom he read avidly from his earliest childhood on. In 1928 he published his first collection of poetry. In 1929 he collaborated in the creation of a poetry journal, and later that year moved to Paris where he established relations with poets and painters of the surrealist school including Aragon, Breton, Dali and Eluard. In 1930 he was involved in the attack by a group of surrealists on the Maldoror bar in Paris, which they felt was disrespectful to an important precursor of the surrealist movement, the nineteenth century poet Lautréamont; Char was stabbed in the course of the fight. In 1932 he married Georgette Goldstein. Following the German occupation he moved back to his native Vaucluse region and joined the Resistance movement.

In the spring of 1943, the Vaucluse Resistance network had been instrumental in providing to the

Lyon maquis information about a large shipment of arms that was scheduled to be transferred at Lyon's Brotteaux train station to German army trucks for distribution throughout the south. A maquis ambush, daringly pulled off in the middle of the afternoon outside the train station in Lyon, had resulted in the deaths of nineteen German soldiers, and the capture by the maquis of hundreds of rifles and thousands of grenades. German reprisals on the citizens of Lyon were bloody, but the success of the operation had done much to raise the morale of the Resistance movement and to undermine the myth of German invincibility. One of the most heartening results of the successful ambush was a sharp spike in the number of Resistance recruits drawn to the cause by the daring success of the Lyon Brotteaux train station raid.

On June 7, 1943, it was Jacques Friedland's turn to carry information about parachute drops in the region to Resistance fighters in Apt, eleven kilometers from Roussillon. At three-thirty that afternoon, as he was leaving Apt to return home to Roussillon, he was arrested by the German Gestapo.

CHAPTER SEVEN

*"Gazing straight before me...through
the windscreen, into the void."*

Following the meeting of the Roussillon maquis,
Pauline Algoud met with Félix Arnaud, Richard
Rosendale, and Samuel Beckett. Algoud argued
that there was no way to bring any help at all to
Jacques while he was in the prison camp at Les
Milles, but that the train traveling through the
mountains between Aix and Lyon was potentially
vulnerable. The train's progress through the
mountains would be slow; train engineers had
learned to be watchful for sabotaged rails, and
rarely exceeded fifty kilometers per hour so that the
train's stopping distance would not exceed the view
of the tracks provided by powerful searchlights on
the front of the locomotive. Algoud suggested they
focus on strategies that would permit at least one of
them to infiltrate the train, while the others followed

its path towards Paris, and assured them that they could count on receiving helpful and accurate information about the train's progress thanks to the excellent communications among the maquis groups in the mountains.

There was an awkward moment when they needed to confront once again the obvious question of the wisdom of putting the three of them and undoubtedly others at risk to try to save one colleague. But the discussion on that point was short. Beyond the principle of loyalty to a colleague in danger, there was the risk that Jacques under duress might inadvertently compromise the Vaucluse maquis. There was also the tremendous propaganda potential to be gleaned from the snatching of a prisoner from under the noses of the Gestapo, as well as the real possibility of ultimately freeing more than one prisoner and disrupting the prisoner transport network.

Richard Rosendale, Sam Beckett and Félix Arnaud agreed to meet at three a.m. to drive to the city of Gap in the Alps. Richard arrived early at the meeting point on the north side of Roussillon, a densely decorated square with greenery, flower boxes, a small pond, the statue of a former maréchal of France killed by a cannon on a nineteenth century battlefield, grass, and benches, all crowded together so thickly that amidst the growing fog, Richard was immediately seized with a sense of claustrophobia. After waiting several minutes, he wandered off to look for Arnaud or Beckett. He returned to the square at three-fifteen, and, still finding no one, was about to go off again in search of them when he thought he saw the silhouette of Arnaud disappearing in the fog to his left. He started to run after him, when a light whistle from over his right shoulder alerted him to the presence of Samuel Beckett, who glared at him and whispered to him to stay put until Arnaud returned with the car.

They took off in the maquis' 2CV Citroen from Roussillon heading for Gap, a 150 kilometer trip which they could make in approximately three hours through back roads. For about an hour, as they drove through the darkness and the fog, the men proposed and discussed different strategies for boarding and following the prisoner train. When they all felt comfortable that they had the outline of a workable plan, Beckett stared sharply at Richard, and asked him why he had not been on time at their rendezvous point in the crowded square. Richard protested that he had in fact been there early, and not seeing them had wandered off to look for them when the precise meeting time had passed. Beckett seemed surprisingly interested in the mechanism of their almost failed meeting:

"Oh, I see. You arrive early, we aren't there, so after five minutes you set off to look for us. We then arrive, and not finding you, set off to look for you."

"Pretty pathetic, isn't it?"

"Well, potentially it is very funny. One could imagine a whole series of failed meetings of characters who had agreed to meet at a specific time in a specific place, but who wander off as you did."

"Who would want to imagine that?"

"A comic novelist or playwright, short on imagination."

"Part of the story of Mr. Watt?"

"I don't think so. Watt is too serious. No, I am thinking of two other clown-like characters setting off on a picaresque adventure."

"It doesn't sound like they are going to get very far."

"No, probably not. Just trying to understand the mechanism of their failed meeting will keep them riveted for quite some time."

"They're thinkers too?"

"Well, they are talkers."

"What do they talk about?"

"Unfortunately, everything that passes through their heads, and since everything they encounter in their life passes through their heads—without necessarily any impact—they are never short of things to talk about. They see time as something to fill, and words as an apt medium to fill it. But their banter is not as empty as their heads. Their words give weight, beauty, even meaning to the impressions that pass through them."

"But they remain totally unconscious?"

"Not totally. They have vague hopes, dreams and aspirations. They expect...maybe expect is too strong to express it...the subtle difference in French between the verbs *attendre* and *s'attendre*—they don't expect something so much as they wait for it."

"Which is not so different from us."

"Perhaps. What are you thinking?"

"Do we really expect our resistance efforts to make a difference? Do we expect to defeat the Germans? Do we expect that France will ever be France again?" Richard pointed to Arnaud: "Félix is the only one of us three who is French, and that only by adoption. Sam, why do you and I stay here and fight for a country that is not ours, against an enemy we know we can't defeat?"

Beckett paused a minute and then, "I know I would rather be at war in France than at peace in my native Ireland. And, as far as the ultimate outcome of our struggle is concerned...well, like my clowns, I don't really expect anything, but I hope and I wait...and in the meantime, I try to find meaning in resistance. As you suggest, Richard, we are perhaps very much like my clowns."

Just before dawn, the 2CV pulled up in front of a collapsing barn four kilometers outside of Gap. A young man with a lantern came out warily, but when he recognized the car and the three passengers, he greeted them warmly, led them inside, offered them bread and cheese, and opened a bottle of wine. The man's name was Georges Pinteau; he was a blacksmith who provided valuable mechanical and technical support to the Gap area maquis. Gasoline rationing under the occupation forced people to rely on horses for work and transportation, and so Pinteau's shop was always busy and became a natural listening post for gathering information from throughout the area. He could repair almost anything, including weapons. He eagerly offered to furnish whatever Beckett, Arnaud and Rosendale needed, and to gather information about the progress of the prisoner train which would be leaving later that day from Les Milles. He urged the three of them to eat and rest while he and his colleagues spent the day finding out what they could. Arnaud gave him a list of supplies he expected they would need: chisels, hammers, small crowbars, pistols, bullets, rope, compasses, knives, flashlights and canteens.

AN INTERVIEW WITH ANDRÉ PATRI

"Do not imagine, because I am
silent, that I am not present."

Paul Schwartz: Today is July 23, 1957, and I am sitting in the office of André Patri, who is a reporter for the Paris daily newspaper, l'*Aurore*. I will be interviewing him about his work as a journalist. Good morning, André, how are you today?

AP: Fine, thank you. And you?

Paul: Fine, thanks. And I thank you for your willingness to participate in this interview; I remind you that this is part of a series of interviews we are doing with French people in various professions, to be used in conversation and culture classes for American students learning French. We will be talking into a tape recorder.

AP: That is fine. What would you like to know?

Paul: Well, let's start by having you tell us a bit about *l'Aurore*: what kind of paper is it?

AP: It is one of four major daily newspapers in Paris. We recently did a survey to determine what features our readers are particularly interested in, and we found that they want us to focus on politics, entertainment, and world events.

Paul: Does the paper have a particular political orientation?

AP: It is generally considered to be a right wing paper, but we never hesitate to criticize inappropriate decisions and pronouncements by political leaders, no matter what position they represent. We never hesitate to criticize De Gaulle for example.

Paul: I see.

AP: And on the desk where I work, arts, radio and television, the political orientation of the paper is unimportant.

Paul: Yes.

AP: And I don't think that it is really that important that a journalist share the political orientation of the newspaper for which he works.

Paul: Yes, I see. What kind of training did you have before entering the field of journalism?

AP: I don't think one needs any special kind of training to be a journalist. It is usually enough to be generally well educated and to be able to read and write, and then being able to type is particularly useful.

Paul: Hmm. That is very different from the American perspective, where the training is very specific. How long have you been working for *l'Aurore?*

AP: Only about five years this time around. I worked for them briefly also twenty years ago in the thirties.

Paul: You were a journalist for *l'Aurore* in the

'30s, did something else for fifteen years, and then came back?

AP: That's right. Incidentally, people around here don't exactly know that. I thought I could talk with you about things that I don't really want people here to know, since you are going to take this back to the US, and it will never be published here.

Paul: Of course. Your present colleagues don't know that you worked for the paper back in the '30s?

AP: No, not at all. The paper has had an almost complete turnover in personnel. And besides...I have changed my name since then.

Paul: Really?

AP: Yes, when I worked for the paper back in the '30s, my name was Raymond Crosatier?

Paul: Why did you change your name?

AP: Well, it's all related to why I quit the paper, and left Paris. You see, I got involved in a deal that...uh...came to the attention of the police, and when it began to come to light, it was a good idea for me to change my name and leave town. So, in 1937, I left Paris for the Midi and changed my name from Raymond Crosatier to André Patri. When I came back to work on this paper after the war, no one remembered Raymond Crosatier, and in fact there was practically no one left around who could have remembered him.

Paul: What can you tell me about the "deal."

AP: Oh, everything; in fact, I have written it all down as a narrative I am trying to get published. It's called "L'Art de Vivre;" you can read it if you want.

Paul: Maybe I will. But tell me about it.

AP: Well, it's mainly about a deal, a caper, that a friend of mine, Richard Rosendale, and I dreamed up. Do you know him?

Paul: No.

AP: I thought you might, since he is an American artist living in Paris.

Paul: No, I haven't met him yet.

AP: Anyway, this was back in '37. I was freelancing, but getting regular work for *l'Aurore* and *le Figaro*, especially for their arts pages. I went to cover a gallery opening of a sculpture show Richard had at a small St-Germain gallery. Since he was a friend, I thought I had a good shot at pushing his show.

Paul: Where had you met?

AP: At the university. I was a studying literature at the same time Richard was enrolled in the Beaux-Arts School. We had some common friends there, as I preferred hanging out with artists rather than the very middle class careerists who were studying literature at the Sorbonne. He had a very dry sense of humor, and then he was involved in some really crazy stunts.

Paul: Like what?

AP: Like hanging a real cadaver he had gotten from some med school friends on the crucifix at Saint Sulpice on Easter morning!

Paul: Yeah, I see. So, tell me about your deal with him.

AP: Hmm, I hadn't seen the connection before, but there is a common theme here. So, getting back to Richard's gallery show: it was a total bust—not many people showed up, and zero sales. And that despite a very clever article I got into the paper about it.

Paul: What was he exhibiting?

AP: Sculptures. Bronze pieces, mostly non-representational small works, almost all of which had feathers attached. He called the exhibit, "Feathered Friends." They were interesting, but overall rather dreary.

Paul: I can see why the public might not have been particularly attracted.

AP: Right. At any rate, despite some pretty good publicity, practically no one came except a few friends of Richard and of the gallery. And then Richard and I went out drinking together a day or two after the unsuccessful opening, and gradually, this really incredible situation developed from that evening, that made Richard famous, and made me sneak out of town and change my name.

Paul: That is intriguing.

AP: And it was the kind of thing that you can't say it was my idea or Richard's idea, it just sort of developed on its own, like it was the idea that developed itself, and just used us for its own purposes.

Paul: Interesting.

AP: It started with our frustration over Richard's lack of success, which got us scheming about ways to attract attention to his work. We at first were just joking about the old cliché of the artist becoming famous and his work selling only after his death, and if the death is a suicide, so much the better. Then after a few more drinks, we were trying to imagine how to stage a fake suicide. We were down on the quay, when all of a sudden we saw something at the edge of the river that made it all seem possible.

Paul: What was that?

AP: A dead body.

Paul: Really?

AP: Yes, as unlikely as it seems, there it was, half submerged, and very decayed, but distinctly human, and very dead.

Paul: So you put Richard's clothes and wallet on him, and set him adrift?

AP: That was the first thought, but then it got much more interesting.

Paul: How's that?

AP: Well, here is where it is not clear where the ideas came from, but we started imagining the ramifications if we made people think the body was me, and that Richard had killed me.

Paul: Why would he do that?

AP: He wouldn't really, but the article I had written about his show was rather ambiguous, and in the course of the evening a lot of people had seen and heard us shouting at each other as we got into one of our old arguments about the esthetic versus the philosophical underpinnings of great art.

Paul: So people might have imagined that he resented your ambiguous article, and that you were shouting at each other about that until he killed you.

AP: Right.

Paul: So how does that advance Richard's career that people think he's a murderer?

AP: Exactly. And so, the plot develops in the following way. At first, people think the body is Richard's, that he killed himself out of despair, and people are attracted by the sad story, go see his art, and buy it from feelings that are one part sentimentality and one part speculation.

Paul: OK.

AP: And then someone tips off the police that it was not Richard, but Raymond Crosatier who was dead in the Seine, and that he and Richard had been shouting at each other all night. And the story makes the first page of *France Soir* several nights in a row, with speculation that Richard killed the journalist, then masked it as his own suicide, and people want to buy Rosendale statues to get in on this developing scandal.

Paul: And is that the way it unfolded?

AP: You bet!

Paul: And how Richard became wealthy and famous, and why you had to change your name and get out of town. But...what was in it for you?

AP: At the beginning that wasn't clear. Remember this is not something we had thought through and planned over time. It was like a spur of the moment act, fueled to a great extent by a night of drinking. But Richard's success was ultimately good for me. I moved with him and his girlfriend Martine to Vence; they gave me a room in the hotel they were able to buy there, and fed me. I was free to write, which is what I had always wanted. I had a good life for three years.

Paul: Then, what happened?

AP: You might remember that there was a war.

Paul: Yes, of course. How did that change things?

AP: Completely. Richard and Martine sold the hotel in Vence, and moved to Roussillon where they bought another, and joined the Resistance movement in the Vaucluse. I decided that Roussillon was too isolated for me, so I packed up my few belongings and joined the French émigré community in London.

Paul: Did you have any connections with those people?

AP: Yes, thanks to one of Richard's associates. When he bought the hotel in Vence, he had the financial backing of a wealthy Parisian named d'Anglade. Believe it or not, Richard had met him when he was briefly jailed for my murder. D'Anglade's wife moved to London, and she and other well positioned French people helped me get set up. I was useful to them, because, as I hope you can see, I speak and write English fairly well.

Paul: Very well.

AP: And that ultimately permitted me to earn a living and contribute to the Resistance cause. I began by giving English lessons to the French living in London, and helping them with their official documents, and other translation needs. But then I was later officially employed by the Free France War Ministry in their communication service. I became an official translator and interpreter, and eventually became proficient at coding and decoding messages that crossed the Channel between London and Resistance units located around France.

Paul: So you spent all the war years in London?

AP: I came back to France occasionally, on missions.

Paul: Sounds dangerous.

AP: It often was. Aviation has always been a passion of mine, and I had a pilot's license, and many hours of flight experience. So I flew myself and others into remote areas of both the occupied and the free zones.

Paul: And then after the war, you came back to Paris?

AP: Yes, and in fact I had a government job for the first few months, but got tired of politics, and decided to focus on what really interested me, writing.

Paul: Journalism?

AP: Yes, to the extent that I needed something that paid me enough to live on, so I could continue writing creatively.

Paul: And have you continued to write creatively?

AP: Oh, yes. I have written two novels, and a number of plays.

Paul: Tell me about them.

AP: I already mentioned one of the novels, called "L'Art de Vivre." It's the one about Richard Rosendale, and our scheme to make him famous.

Paul: Oh, yeah. Unpublished I think you said.

AP: Like everything I have written.

Paul: Oh, too bad.

AP: And then, there is the sequel to that novel. I mentioned Richard's work with the Resistance during the war years? He has been working with me on a narrative that is nearly complete; it tells that story.

Paul: Why haven't you been able to get them published?

AP: It's just hard for an unknown author to break into print. Maybe after I'm dead...

CHAPTER EIGHT

"We all know your station is the best kept of the entire network, but there are times when that is not enough."

It had been a relatively easy matter for members of the Gap Resistance network to learn from colleagues working for the railroad where and when the prisoner train from Les Milles would be making stops to pick up additional prisoners and guards. When Georges Pinteau reported to them that there was a scheduled stop around midnight in Lyon where additional boxcars filled with prisoners would be added, Rosendale, Beckett and Arnaud agreed that this would probably be the best opportunity for them to board the train. But late in the morning, just as they were about to leave for Lyon, Pinteau received a report that at the train's third stop at the smaller station in Vienne, scheduled tentatively for eleven p.m., two additional prisoners and their guard would be boarding the train. They decided to begin their operation in Vienne.

As they drove up to Vienne through the afternoon, they worked on creating potential plans of action based on the broad outlines they had earlier developed, subtly diverging scenarios which would continue to evolve as events beyond their control unfolded. Each scenario began with one of them in a gendarme uniform holding one or two of the others prisoner. Building on these six initial situations, all three contributed to imagining the complex series of events triggered by foreseeable and unforeseeable events which might lead them towards dozens of possible denouements. Beckett carefully recorded the scenarios in his notebook. They also reviewed subtle hand signals through which they could communicate without drawing attention.

When they arrived at the Vienne train station at about seven p.m., Arnaud in civilian clothes and a fake moustache entered the station while the two others waited in the car. He quickly noted the layout of the station, while pretending to study the departure board, and left again avoiding eye contact with anyone. He then walked to the café across from the station and conferred briefly with its proprietor, a Resistance sympathizer who had been alerted to expect Arnaud's visit in the course of the evening. Arnaud, Rosendale and Beckett then drove back out of town, stopped on an isolated farm road to discuss their options, and ultimately settled on a plan that began with Richard Rosendale and Félix Arnaud in gendarme uniforms, and Sam Beckett dressed as a prisoner.

And so, at ten-thirty on the night of June 9, two men in the uniforms of captains in the Gendarmerie strode into the Vienne train station with a scared looking prisoner. One of the captains pushed the prisoner roughly onto an empty seat next to two other handcuffed prisoners already seated there, and warmly greeted the young gendarme guarding them.

Lieutenant Frédéric Tallier of the Gendarmerie Nationale had always considered himself to be one of the most unremarkable men on earth. Born in 1920, in a working class southern suburb of Paris, his family, his friends, his surroundings, his education and his temperament all seemed to predestine him to follow in the footsteps of his father Alphonse, who had worked his way gradually, by dint of unquestioning dedication and self-effacement, into a lifelong assembly line position in the engine manufacturing plant of Renault in Boulogne-Billancourt. Frédéric's schooling had been practical and technical. Without excelling in any way, he had nonetheless passed his exams, usually on the second or third try, and at the age of sixteen, he was granted the technical certificate which was the necessary and sufficient document for the lifetime appointment he aspired to under the paternalistic aegis of Renault.

Frédéric had been briefly mobilized in the hasty preparations for war with Germany. Following the devastating defeat of the French army, he had hoped to return to his post with Renault. But when it became obvious that able-bodied Frenchmen were being rounded up by the Germans and shipped to labor camps in Germany, Frédéric applied for a position in the Gendarmerie, which appeared to offer an alternative that would allow him to limit the impact of world events on his modest personal aspirations. Forced nonetheless to move to the garrison in Lyon, away from the warmth of his family's modest apartment, and—most distressingly—away from the very enjoyable company of Mlle Thérèse Angiot whom he had been conscientiously courting, Frédéric suddenly became conscious that although he loved his country and Marshall Pétain, he perhaps loved his family, his security, and certainly his Thérèse even more. He never articulated the phrase, "This isn't fair," but some sentiment analogous to that thought knotted his stomach at times.

Throughout training, he had just barely succeeded in gaining basic police skills, without attracting any notice for exceptional or even unexceptional accomplishments. He got by. Through unremarkable and faithful service, and a blind trust in the officers who tried to mold him, he gained the rank of lieutenant, and in that capacity was given the responsibility to take two prisoners to the train station in Vienne on that night in June, and to accompany them on the train ride to Paris.

Very conscious of his unremarkableness, and his lack of social skills, and eagerly seeking approval and recognition from those who seemed more remarkable, and who had social skills, he was charmed and flattered by the attention of one of the captains who greeted him warmly that night at the Vienne train station.

"Hello. Good evening! They've given us another prisoner for you; I hope you don't mind."

"Uh, no one told me about this, but if you say so,

I have no problem taking another one. He looks harmless enough."

"Good! By the way, they told me in town that the train is delayed at least forty minutes. It won't get here before eleven-thirty."

"What's the problem? Do you know?"

"A terrorist attack, between Montélimar and Valence. Their usual tactics: a cow on the track, so the train slows down, and a bunch of ruffians come running out shooting, then disappear back into the woods. Several gendarmes tried to follow them, but of course they had all disappeared."

"It is so barbaric and primitive!"

"You said it! Say, can I buy you a drink? My colleague here can keep an eye on our prisoners."

"Certainly, Captain! There is a café across the way."

The "colleague," Richard Rosendale, smiled and nodded as the two gendarmes strode out of the station, arm in arm, joking about the clumsiness of the terrorist operation, as they went into the café across from the station which Arnaud had visited earlier in the evening.

Richard sat down facing the prisoners, warily eyeing them. No one said a word. Other travelers coming into the station saw a gendarme guarding three French prisoners, and quickly sized up the situation. Some sneered at Richard, and smiled sympathetically at the prisoners. Richard heard one old woman spit contemptuously into the street as she left the station.

At eleven o'clock, Félix Arnaud, still dressed as a gendarme, strode back into the station alone, and dismissed Richard with a nod and an awkward wave. Twenty-five minutes later, when the train arrived, Arnaud herded his three prisoners into car #23, relieving the guard who had accompanied them from Les Milles.

Jacques Friedland's astonishment at finding himself face to face with Félix Arnaud and Sam Beckett was replaced by a rapid series of reflections that left him, in quick succession, elated, frightened, remorseful and ultimately filled with awe and exhilaration. The joyful realization that Arnaud and Beckett were there to rescue him had just sunk in when he was overwhelmed by the tremendous risk that these valuable members of the Resistance were taking. His gratitude at their spontaneous leap into the belly of the whale was tempered by the fear that his capture could ultimately lead to the deaths of additional comrades. But as he watched and waited and noted that Beckett and Arnaud made no immediate move to neutralize the other guard in the train car, he gradually came to understand that their goal extended perhaps far beyond the release of captured Resistance member Jacques Friedland, that Arnaud's strategic imagination had led him to conceive Jacques' capture as the first step in a daring infiltration of a prisoner train which could have dramatic positive results for the Resistance movement. Three maquisards, two of them armed— Jacques assumed that Sam Beckett had at least a pistol in the oversized trousers he was wearing—in the car of a prisoner train headed to Paris presented a world of opportunities. Jacques closed his eyes.

He awoke as the train came to a jerky, screeching stop; he had no idea how long they had been traveling, or how long he might have slept. Within minutes the door of the boxcar swung open, and they were greeted by German soldiers who firmly and quickly herded all of the prisoners out of the train car. The early morning was grey and drizzly. Through the fog, Jacques could see they were in a train station in a nondescript northern French town which he assumed must be Drancy. As they assembled in groups in the street in front of the station, a guard barked out in heavily accented

French that they were in Drancy, and would be held at the Drancy Transit Camp, pending "processing." They were then marched at a rapid pace through the town to the prison complex.

The Drancy prison, named after the northeastern suburb of Paris in which it was located, was originally planned in the 1930s as a large, U-shaped, multi-story, public housing project. It was converted into a detention center for prisoners of war by the Vichy government of Marshall Pétain in 1941. In August, 1941, the French police raided Paris's 11th *arrondissement* and rounded up 4,232 Jews living in the district. At first they were imprisoned under miserable conditions in the Paris velodrome, but later transferred to Drancy. From that point on, the facility at Drancy became a major detention centre, primarily for Jews, but also others labeled as "undesirables." During the spring of 1942, the Germans began systematic deportations of Jews from Drancy to extermination camps in occupied Poland. Between the summer of 1942 and July 31, 1944, all but twelve of the seventy-nine deportation trains, carrying approximately 65,000 Jews to the east, left from Drancy. Originally under the control of the French police, the camp's day to day control passed into the hands of the Gestapo in

1943, when SS officer Alois Brunner became camp commandant as part of the major stepping up at all facilities for mass exterminations. French gendarmes provided guards, but on the eve of the departure of deportation trains, representatives of the Commissioner for Jewish Affairs, who reported directly to the Ministry of the Interior, arrived at the camp to take charge of the searching of passengers and loading them onto the trains, at which point they were turned over to German guards.

From the beginning, there were disagreements among French authorities over who had internal responsibility for conditions within the camp, and as a result only minimal efforts were made for prisoners' comfort. When 4,232 Jews rounded up in the August 1942 raids were imprisoned at Drancy, there were only frames for 1200 bunk beds, and as many as forty or fifty prisoners were assigned to a room. Food was inadequate and unhealthy, based on a steady diet of cabbage soup. In the fall of 1942, there was a serious outbreak of dysentery, with a high mortality rate; as many as 950 prisoners may have died. A French intelligence report on conditions in the camp in December 1942 concluded, "Those who have not with their own eyes seen some of those released from Drancy can only have a faint idea of the wretched state of internees in this camp which is unique in history. It is said that the notorious camp of Dachau is nothing in comparison with Drancy."

Members of the Resistance were well informed about the prison camps, and Jacques knew the story of the thousands of Jews rounded up in the 1942 raid, their detention at Drancy, and eventual transport to camps outside of France where they presumably died. As they approached the ominous building, the sight of it combined with his knowledge of the 1942 raids and arrests filled him with dread and discouragement. He thought of Joanne, thought of his friends, and his eyes filled with tears. But then, through the drifting fog, he caught site of the Paris skyline off in the distance. The dome of Sacré Coeur was dimly visible, and, remembering his life and adventures in Paris with Joanne and Richard and Martine, he found a sudden strength in the joyful certainty that somehow he would get out of this, that he would eventually be reunited with his friends, and that someday Paris would once again be Paris. In the meantime, he had to do what he could to survive, and to keep hoping. The presence of Sam Beckett, with whom he had not yet exchanged a word, was a further comfort.

Beckett and Friedland were shown into a cell with a dozen other prisoners. Some daylight penetrated through the barred door, and between passages of the guards, it was possible to converse. In quickly whispered phrases, Beckett told Jacques what had been done so far. He had no sure information about the next steps, but was able to assure Jacques that Richard Rosendale and Félix Arnaud would be meeting with highly placed figures in the Paris Resistance, planning a dramatic blow at the prisoner transport network towards the camps in Poland, and that Resistance units throughout eastern France would be mobilized for the effort.

Chapter Nine

*"Just concentrate on putting
one foot before the next."*

Félix Arnaud, after having turned over his
prisoners, watched as they were led into a cell, then
slipped out of the prison and headed on foot to the
Drancy train station. In a bathroom stall, he
removed his gendarme uniform, and carefully
wrapped it in a large piece of Kraft paper he had
folded into his breast pocket, and neatly taped the
package.

Dressed in unremarkable civilian clothes, and
carrying a package under his arm, Arnaud melted
confidently into the crowd buying tickets and
boarding the commuter train to Paris at ten o'clock
on the morning of Thursday, June 10, 1943. He got
off at the Gare du Nord and walked to the Hôtel de
Maubeuge, a modest but comfortable hotel a block
from the station, where he had arranged to meet

Richard. Checking in at the hotel, he assumed a light Mexican accent; the hotel clerk glanced at his Mexican passport, added his name to the register, and assigned him a room on the third floor. Richard arrived two hours later, and the two went out to lunch together, and ate mussels and French fries with a light Belgian beer, at a brasserie near the hotel. Over lunch, they discussed their next steps, speaking quietly, in English.

Their loose plans had to be supported with minute by minute details, and they had to act fast. Jacques would be on a train to Auschwitz within days, and it would be only a matter of hours before the prison authorities noticed that they had a prisoner, Samuel Beckett, with no formal arrest documents. Beckett was prepared to protest that his arrest was a mistake and to produce an Irish passport in the name of Milo O'Shea. But if any prison officials recognized him as a wanted member of the Resistance, or if they happened to search him and found his gun, he could face an immediate firing squad, despite his eloquence, cool-headedness, and lightning quick ability to calculate and invent.

Members of the Paris Resistance movement were highly motivated by the possibility suddenly presented to them to disrupt the passage of a prisoner train from Drancy to Auschwitz. The presence within one car of that train of armed Resistance fighters was perceived by the local network as a dramatic and propitious opportunity, one on which to build a major operation through which they could demonstrate to the world that the French Resistance was alive, well-organized, and willing to risk many lives to save imprisoned Jews, and to defy the seemingly insurmountable German mechanism of death.

Richard had a special relationship with one of the most powerful members of the Parisian Resistance Council. Before he left Paris for Vence in 1937, Richard had met under very peculiar conditions the disgraced judge, Baron Olivier d'Anglade, who had subsequently supported Richard and his wife Martine in the acquisition and renovation of the Miramar Hotel in Vence.

At the time of the fall of Paris, d'Anglade had resisted the temptation to move to England with his wife. He sent her to London, but he himself remained and rallied around the new government of Marshall Pétain with feigned enthusiasm. The Marshall's staff, enthusiastically overlooking the somewhat mysterious stain on Olivier's formerly brilliant record as judge, appointed him to a highly responsible position in the office of the Ministry of the Interior of the Vichy government.

From that vantage point, d'Anglade often found himself in the impossible position of having to defend during his daytime working hours the masquerade of Vichy justice, so that at other times he was perfectly placed to work clandestinely against that government's hypocrisy and baseness. Often forced to overlook individual government crimes against humanity so that he could support the organized resistance to that government and the German occupation, Olivier's nighttime dreams were haunted by his acquiescence in the punishment inflicted on loyal French men and women, so that he could help maintain the hopes of those same captured patriots through his invaluable support of their cause.

At that very moment, he was the Ministry of the Interior's legal liaison in Paris with the German prisoner of war hierarchy. On the basis of his impeccable legal credentials and a well earned reputation for loyalty, knowledge and integrity, he had been officially charged by the Vichy government with the responsibility to monitor the transfer of prisoners from the Gendarmerie to the

Gestapo, and to certify to the extent possible German compliance with accepted international standards of prisoner treatment. Olivier had little bargaining leverage with the Nazi high command; he occasionally gained some measure of humane treatment for prisoners, but was powerless to even slow the relentless mechanism of genocide. He was anguished to acknowledge that his very presence gave to the process a semblance of official respectability.

On the other hand, he had contributed substantially to the few brilliant successes of the Resistance movement against the deportation process—without arousing any suspicion of his role. The Gendarmerie and the Gestapo trusted him with detailed information concerning prisoner train movements. On six occasions he had fed that information to strike forces within the Resistance movement, and had worked with their leaders to develop attack strategies which risked few lives, and saved optimal numbers of prisoners, while preserving the security of his position. One of his most satisfying successes was the September 1942 escape of fifty Jewish children from a deportation train headed for Auschwitz. Loved, respected, and admired by the dozen or so members of the network who knew him as Maximilien, his real identity and position were known to none of them.

At six o'clock on the evening of June 10, a distinguished looking man in a dark suit walked up to the blue front door of 110 rue de Charenton near the Gare de Lyon. He unlocked the door, entered the small courtyard, climbed one flight of stairs and knocked three times, then two times, on the door of the apartment to the right of the stairway. The door was opened and Olivier d'Anglade entered the small sparsely furnished living room of a neat one bedroom apartment. Félix Arnaud and Richard Rosendale were there waiting for him, and greeted him warmly. Arnaud quickly outlined the series of events that had brought them to Paris with Friedland and Beckett who were now prisoners at Drancy.

D'Anglade announced worriedly, "They will be shipped out with the next train for Auschwitz, scheduled to leave Saturday afternoon. That gives us very little time to work out details of an escape attempt." He went on thoughtfully, "And I've got to create an arrest record for Beckett that will be on the desk of the prison commandant tomorrow morning. Not a problem, but tell me more about him."

Richard provided details of Beckett's recent Resistance work in Roussillon as well as his previous work with the Resistance in Paris that had led to his near arrest two years earlier, and then added that he is a novelist.

"What kind of novels does he write? Anything likely to provoke the Germans?"

"Perhaps, as there is a persistent irreverent and scatological tone to much of his work. He has actually published only one novel, *Murphy*, which came out in England in '38, and in Paris in '39."

"What is it about?"

"It is hard to answer that succinctly. It is short but complicated and sometimes obscure. It is basically a comic novel about an Irishman named Murphy, who lives in London with a former streetwalker named Celia. The couple is pursued by a trio of other Irishmen, one of whom is in love with Celia, as well as by an Irishwoman who is in love with Murphy."

"Is he a noble character?"

"Not at all. Totally unmotivated and solipsistic, his greatest pleasure is to tie himself naked in a rocking chair. His great drama is that Celia insists that he get a job or she will resume her life as a streetwalker."

"What becomes of Murphy?"

"He secures a job in a mental institute, where he serves remarkably well as a patients' aide, getting along splendidly with the most deranged of the patients. Until the day when, tied to his rocking chair as the gas comes on in his room, he is burnt almost beyond recognition."

"Almost?"

"His mistress is able to confirm his identity by means of the wine colored birthmark on his right buttock."

"Good. Based on what you describe, we can fabricate an arrest warrant for Samuel Beckett on charges of moral decadence, related to the publication of scatological literature. We can predate the warrant to coincide with his previous residence in Paris, with no mention of the more dangerous accusations against him. Is Beckett prepared to help orchestrate an escape plan?"

"Absolutely. We have created scenarios designed to get as many as two hundred prisoners off the train between Drancy and the German border. He awaits word from me that we have official approval to proceed, and then based on the information we can get about the train logistics—length, speed, schedule, material conditions of the cars, and the number of prisoners—he will work out the details of a plan that the four of us will execute."

"OK. Tomorrow morning, you must get word to Beckett that they will be shipped out the following day, that he has the approval of the Paris Resistance Council, and that he will be given the information he needs in the course of the day, and additional assistance later on. Then, meet me at three o'clock in front of the Sainte-Chapelle. Look for a black Citroen sedan with official plates, and climb in the back seat. I will be able to give you then the information you need."

From the meeting on the rue de Charenton, d'Anglade walked back to his office. Using file information and the details he had received from Arnaud and Rosendale, he was able to create a 1940 arrest warrant for Samuel Beckett. Getting it into the file folder on the desk of the commandant at Drancy would have been difficult, but fortunately for d'Anglade, one of his former personal servants, Joseph Brunot, was employed as a secretary within the Prison Administration—a post which d'Anglade's influence had made possible—and had access to confidential files. By means of a quick late night call to Brunot, d'Anglade was able to assure that the newly created Beckett warrant would be in the proper file in the morning.

In his official capacity, d'Anglade had access to much of the information that would be helpful to support the escape attempt. He could justifiably demand from the prison commandant's staff that he be given for humanitarian reasons the list of prisoners to be deported, the nature of the train, and even the names and number of prisoners to be assigned to each train car. But for other practical details, he needed the help of railroad employees committed to the Resistance cause. Under his Resistance pseudonym Maximilien, d'Anglade sent out an urgent appeal through the Paris Resistance network for specific information about the cars that would make up the train scheduled to leave Saturday afternoon: the construction materials, their age, their dimensions and layout, and then also information about the route, including stops along the way, anticipated speed between stations, and times of arrival at each stop.

CHAPTER TEN

"If this train were never to move
again I should not greatly mind."

Just after one o'clock on the afternoon of
Saturday, June 12, the quiet gloom of the Drancy
prison was interrupted by sharp sounds, loud
voices giving orders, doors being opened noisily,
thuds and occasional wails of pain. Prisoners were
being marched out. French police, with a few
German soldiers visible among them, armed with
machine guns and pistols, were yelling at prisoners,
forcing them to their feet, pushing them out of their
cells, and marching them down the corridors of the
prison building, out into the courtyard. When a
group of seventy prisoners had been assembled,
other German soldiers with more machine guns
and pistols marched them out into the street,
through the center of town to the railroad station.
The prisoners were forced to move at nearly a run;

several who fell, men, women and children, were roughly kicked, pushed to their feet, and forced along the cobblestone streets. In the railroad yard, they were herded into wooden train cars, about seventy people per car.

Richard Rosendale had arrived at the Drancy train station just before one o'clock, dressed as a government employee; and with the diplomatic ID, briefcase, and pass which d'Anglade had provided was able to move to a position on the quay of track number six from which the prisoner train was to leave. He had been standing there for no more than a few minutes when, as they had previously arranged, Arnaud, now in a German army uniform, greeted him warmly and loudly in a German accented French, and invited him to visit one of the prisoner cars. He escorted him into the still empty car number 18. In the deserted car, as Arnaud watched the door, Richard quickly removed his suit and stuffed it into the empty brief case he was carrying. Beneath he was wearing clothing appropriate to a prisoner. Arnaud, now carrying the briefcase, escorted him out the other side of the train car, passed off the brief case to a waiting station employee, and the two joined a group of prisoners who were about to be herded into the same car number 18. Arnaud, who spoke German flawlessly, was easily able to convince and reassure the guard already assigned to remain with the prisoners in that car, that he had been added for extra security as a result of rumors about an expected escape attempt.

Friedland and Beckett had heard the commotion throughout the prison long before guards came to the door of their cell at about one-thirty, and had guessed that they would also soon be herded out into the streets. Like the others before them, they were forced out of their cell, and then led at nearly a running pace towards the train station. At one point in the hurried march through the streets of Drancy, Friedland and Beckett became separated. Beckett, realizing that Friedland was somewhere behind him, managed to duck quickly into a grain storage warehouse just before the train station, and peeked out anxiously waiting for the next group to arrive. Several minutes passed, but finally, to his relief, Beckett was able to spot Friedland in the next group; he was particularly visible because he seemed to be engaged in a heated exchange with another prisoner, a large man who had grabbed Friedland's arm, and was gesturing wildly at the risk of calling unwanted attention to the two of them. Beckett slipped out of the warehouse, and was able to integrate himself unnoticed among the prisoners surrounding Friedland, as the other prisoner released Jacques' arm and melted back into the crowd. The group was stopped in front of a train car which had a stenciled 16 on the outside paneling. The prisoners were crowded in, an armed guard went in with them, snarled at them menacingly, and made them lie or sit on the wooden floor, forced together in an uncomfortable familiarity.

Throughout the afternoon, the prisoners sat and waited. No conversation was tolerated. Sighs and sobs were met with abuse and threats from the guard. All settled into a quiet miserable resignation as afternoon faded into evening, and finally the prisoners felt a jerk, with an unexpected sense of relief, as the train eased into motion. The prisoners felt the train gradually pick up speed as it moved out into the Ile de France countryside east of Paris. At first it moved slowly, with frequent jerky stops, often punctuated with shouted conversations in German or French from somewhere outside the train. About ninety minutes after the train left, there was one prolonged stop. For almost an hour, they waited in silence broken occasionally by hammering noises and unidentifiable metallic screeches. Finally it eased into motion again. Despite their anxiety and discomfort, the prisoners gradually drifted into sleep.

At about two a.m., the guard in car number 16, Wilhelm Gaussen, feeling that his prisoners presented no particular danger, rested his machine gun on the floor between his legs, and leaned back with his head against the end wall of the train. Beckett, while seeming to sleep just a couple of feet away, had been watching closely through half-closed eyes. As the guard's eyelids began to flutter, Beckett prodded Jacques Friedland to his right, who discreetly drew his pistol, concealing it under his arm.

With a quick efficient gesture, Beckett rose and put his two hands on the guard's machine gun, while Jacques put his pistol to the guard's temple. It was all accomplished so quickly that the guard merely grunted in surprise then threw his hands up in the air in surrender. Beckett took the machine gun. He pulled a roll of tape from the pocket of his coat. Before placing a wadded piece of cloth in the guard's mouth, he apologized in polite German. The guard shrugged and muttered, "Don't worry. I don't want to play hero." Beckett gagged and bound him with the tape.

The other prisoners watched in fascinated silence. Beckett was acting out a scenario which had first been developed in the car with Arnaud and Rosendale during the night following Jacques' arrest, and whose official approval was given in the paper he had found folded in his pocket following his interrogation the previous morning. The plan of action he exposed had been further refined on the basis of logistical information about the train that Arnaud had been able to share with him the evening before.

Beckett addressed the prisoners firmly in French:

"We are being taken to the death camp in Auschwitz, Poland, where we will all be gassed to death within forty-eight hours. Our only chance to survive is to escape this train car before it leaves French territory. We have brought tools to remove the wooden floor boards of this train car, so we can slip out underneath the car as it slows for its entry into the station at Metz. That will be in approximately ninety minutes. We will give you very precise instructions."

Beckett produced two chisels, a hammer and a small crowbar from pockets sewn into his clothing, and proceeded to go to work on the floor boards in the center of the train. With Jacques' help and that of one of the other prisoners, a strong and energetic man who had eagerly come forward when the work began, they removed several boards, already softened by age and rot. After they had opened a hole about two feet by three feet, Beckett with a small flashlight peered under the car with his head just inches from the cross ties speeding beneath him at eighty kilometers per hour. When he had fully examined the underbelly of the car, he proceeded to remove several more boards, opening a hole about two feet wide and five feet long. He took one of the boards, and sketched on it a neat but simple diagram of the underside of the car which he held up to the other prisoners:

"Beneath the floor, about five centimeters in front of the opening which we have created, is an iron beam which extends across the car and hangs down about ten centimeters towards the ground. As you descend into the opening, you will brace your toes against that cross bar. If necessary, we can support your upper body with a rope for you must keep your body rigid. With your hands and arms tight against your sides, you will drop swiftly and flat onto the cross ties between the rails. There is about a forty centimeter clearance between the cross bars of the cars and the cross ties of the rails. If you fall perfectly flat, and lie still, the train will pass harmlessly over you. Count the eight cars behind us, then get up and run perpendicularly from the tracks towards the left, for at least five hundred meters, before turning again to the left, so that you will be heading back in the direction from which we came. There will be friends looking for us in the woods. Listen for a double whistle, the first part inhaled, the second part exhaled. Return the same signal. Any questions?"

"What if we don't find anyone waiting for us?"

"Look for any farmhouse, identify yourself as an escaped prisoner, and hope they are patriots. It is your only chance."

Beckett went on, "There are seventy-two of us in this car. There will also be prisoners escaping from another car, probably about the same number. I will assign each of you a number from one to seventy-two." He proceeded to assign numbers, giving the lower numbers to those who appeared to need the most time to flee eventual pursuers or who needed the most help getting through the opening in the floor. He reserved the last two numbers for Jacques and himself. Prisoner number seventy, the last one to leave the car before Friedland and

Beckett, posed a bit of a problem. He was named Stéphane Goldberg, and it was he who had quickly stepped forward to help in the process of removing the floorboards of the train. He was an unusually large and athletic man, by several inches taller than any of the other prisoners, and broader in the shoulders. After having helped to remove the floorboards, he made himself useful in the process of aiding prisoners to escape, working with Beckett to support them as Friedland maneuvered them through the hole in the floor. Because of his size and strength, Beckett had willingly kept him at hand until all of the other prisoners had gone. But now he had to face the reality that the hole would need to be enlarged, and that the man's weight and size would be almost more than he and Friedland could handle as they helped him through the floor of the car. They hurriedly dislodged one additional floorboard from each side of the hole, and then straining against his bulk, lowered him into the opening. As he dropped through, his leg slipped free from Friedland's grasp and smashed a floorboard half of which dangled at the edge of the opening, but he nonetheless fell freely to the tracks.

Two cars further back in the train, Félix Arnaud and Richard Rosendale performed the same tasks and made the same speeches as quickly and efficiently. There too the guard had offered no resistance. Their task was a bit more delicate as there were in their car children as young as twelve years old. But the children proved just as resolute and fearless as the adults, understanding perfectly that their only chance to survive was to follow the detailed instructions of their armed saviors. One by one, the seventy-four prisoners of that car dropped safely through the hole practiced by Richard and Arnaud, who then dropped through the hole themselves, and all were eventually surrounded and herded to safety by members of the eastern France Resistance movement, who had massed in the woods west of Metz for this daring escape.

By seven o'clock on the morning of June 13, 1943, 146 of the 148 occupants of cars 16 and 18 of the prisoner-of-war train from Drancy to Auschwitz which had left the previous night were accounted for, and had been driven in cars and small trucks towards safe havens within the Vosges Mountains, in farms identified as friendly to the Resistance cause. Félix Arnaud and Richard Rosendale, as well as the seventy prisoners of car 16 who had escaped thanks to their perfect execution of the escape plan, waited nervously for word of the fate of Sam Beckett and Jacques Friedland, who were missing in action.

CHAPTER ELEVEN

"...all that fall"

Jacques slipped into the hole in the floor, and braced his feet against the lateral support, as Sam held him up with the rope. He slipped his head back under the floor board, and grabbed the sides of the hole. The train was moving slowly but the noise of the wheels against the tracks was still a modulated shriek. He counted to three, felt the rope relax and dropped. For an agonizing fraction of a second, his right leg was caught by something protruding from the floor of the train, and he screamed, as he thought that his leg was going to be ripped off at the thigh; but the protruding board broke off after inflicting a searing pain through his hip joint.

He gritted his teeth and lay still as the remaining cars passed over him, then painfully rolled over the left rail, trying to ignore the pain which caused him to groan then vomit. He rolled about five meters from the rail bed, then lay still, waiting for help.

Sam Beckett had heard Jacques' cry and knew something had gone wrong. Within seconds after Jacques had dropped through, after a brief ironic salute to the still bound German guard, he braced himself in the hole, calling on all of his strength to stiffen his body, supported only by the lateral leg brace and his hands on the side of the hole. He dropped freely, as Jacques' leg had knocked away the protruding floor board which had remained following Goldberg's escape. After the passage of the eight cars, he nimbly sprang from between the rails, and raced back towards Jacques. He had calculated the speed of the train at about thirty kilometers per hour, and since his drop had come only about one minute after Jacques', he knew that Jacques would be within five hundred meters behind.

He was suddenly aware of a screeching braking noise from the direction of the train. Had the escapes been detected? How long would it take the Germans to mount a pursuit? Beckett knew that he had dropped from the train five to seven kilometers from Metz, and that the train was stopping at a point at least two kilometers ahead of him. The German soldiers on the train, even if they were aware of the escape, would have to continue into Metz to get reinforcements for a serious pursuit of the escaped prisoners. He had time to find Jacques, and get to safety.

He ran at a comfortable pace, and after three or four minutes began calling out to Jacques. He heard a gasping, "I'm here," coming from a grove of trees ahead of him. He raced to the grove and found Jacques sprawled in obvious pain beneath a pine, dimly visible through the moonlit grove.

"What's wrong?"

"My leg, a loose board from the flooring almost tore it off. The hip is dislocated if not completely shattered."

"Can you stand at all?"

"No."

"OK. We still have time. It will be at least an hour before the Germans come through here with their dogs. Let's get moving."

Beckett reasoned that they had no chance of moving to the position five hundred meters from the tracks where the Resistance members would be looking for them. They needed to move as quickly away from the tracks as they could, while at the same time looking to move to a lower elevation where they could hope to find a stream in which they could mask their scent to elude the German dogs which would be on their trail quickly.

They took stock of their possessions: a couple of tins of food, their guns, some bullets, a compass, a water bottle, a knife, the rope, the flashlight, the chisel and hammer, and the clothes they were wearing. The night was mild, so Beckett took off his shirt, and ripped up half of it to bind Jacques' upper legs together which seemed to reduce the pain in his hip. With the rest of his shirt he fashioned a sack in which he tied up their possessions. He had Jacques climb onto his back, and crouched forward, moving at times on all fours, carrying Jacques through the woods, heading west and south, away from the tracks, on a downhill path through the moonlit trees.

They moved along slowly and steadily for about an hour. Beckett gradually became aware of a slight but distinctive sound of rushing water. At almost the same moment when he was convinced that they were indeed approaching a sizeable stream, he heard coming from behind them, still far in the distance, the sound of barking dogs.

Resolutely he scampered and crawled with Jacques still on his back towards the water, straining to hear the dogs and judge their distance and direction of approach. He sensed that they were still many minutes away, when quite suddenly the ground began to give way under his feet, as they entered a rain swollen stream flowing south and west in the direction they were heading.

He gave the sack to Jacques, who now mounted high on his back, while Beckett entered the stream. Beckett was a strong swimmer, but Jacques' weight would have quickly tired him if he tried to swim far. And it was important to keep the sack and its contents out of the water. So, with Jacques on his back, Beckett waded across the stream, then started crawling downstream through the mud on the far bank, still carrying Jacques, often with his face under the water or in the mud, lifting his head every thirty seconds to gulp some air, and to question Jacques breathlessly about his position, the security of the sack, and what noises he detected.

At one point, the dogs had seemed to be gaining on them, but then they had gone off in another direction. Beckett guessed that the pursuers had crossed the stream where they had, but then had continued searching the banks of the stream and the adjoining woods trying to recapture their scent. Sixty minutes of crawling downstream along the muddy bank would put enough distance between them and their pursuers so that they could recross the stream, and make their way through the woods on the opposite side.

At about five a.m., Jacques and Sam stopped in a dense grove of trees to wait for the first light of dawn to break. They ate and drank from the supplies they had brought with them and slept lightly. As the day began to break, they found themselves in a rocky overgrown underbrush. As far as they could see, there were no roads, no dwellings and no fences. They set off in a southwesterly direction with Jacques again mounted helplessly on Beckett's back.

After about ninety minutes of slow progress through the dense underbrush, they came to a clearing at whose far edge stood a small two-story stone dwelling. Beckett left Friedland in the brush at the edge of the clearing, and walked up to the door of the house. He knocked and called. Having no answer, and hearing no movement from within, he shouldered the locked door three times, until it burst open. Inside there were signs of a hurried flight, which had probably taken place months earlier. Dirty, moldy dishes filled the sink. The cupboards still held cans and jars of dry goods.

Beckett went back to the edge of the clearing where he had left Jacques Friedland, and carried him into the house. He placed him on a partially made bed in a corner of the dwelling's main room. A quick look around the house, cellar, attic and grounds persuaded Beckett that they could hold out there for quite some time. The well behind the house still provided fresh water. There were carrots, turnips, onions and potatoes in the cellar, as well as a cask of wine, rice and flour in canisters in the kitchen, and in back of the house was a load of firewood. There was even clothing in a small chest.

The interior of the house was very dim, even as the sun rose in the sky. Two small smoke darkened windows were located high on either side of the room. By climbing on a small stool which had been stored under the table, Beckett could look out through the windows to scan the horizon, which appeared dim through the windows' murky glass. In the attic, Beckett found among other things an old, decrepit but still serviceable wheel chair, which he brought down to give Jacques some degree of mobility.

They spent a fairly comfortable first day and night resting in the house. When Beckett explored the area outside the house the next morning, he found three hundred meters behind it a small stream with a good supply of trout. When he reported this back to Jacques, they agreed that they could survive for a very long time here. They still had two guns and bullets; no doubt they could find rabbits and squirrels to hunt. But how could they get word to their wives, friends and comrades that they had survived the escape?

Beckett set off that afternoon to explore a wider area. After an hour and a half of difficult passage across rugged terrain and through thick underbrush, he spotted what appeared to be another abandoned farmhouse about five kilometers to the south. Many farms throughout occupied France had been abandoned; the women and children who remained after the men were drafted, killed, imprisoned or sent to forced labor had set off in desperation to live with aunts, uncles, sisters and cousins on other farms or in the cities, leaving their homes behind.

This farmhouse showed no sign of life. The door was unlocked, and flapping open. The cupboards had been stripped bare. He noticed a buffet in the corner with a locked cabinet. He sat down on the floor and worked at the lock with his pocket knife. It finally yielded, and inside was a two-way radio, similar to the radio that Richard and Martine kept hidden in the armoire of their hotel dining room. Its battery was dead. Beckett reasoned that there must be a charger somewhere around. He looked through the cellar, and the attic, then went out to the barn. There he found a large tool chest, which after some fumbling he managed to unlock; inside was a hand-crank generator.

He brought the generator into the dwelling and wired it to the radio's battery. After several minutes of cranking, the radio failed to spring to life. At this point, Beckett realized that he needed Jacques Friedland, who had a basic knowledge of electronics, and was also more aware than he of the safe frequencies and coded language through which Resistance members communicated. The radio and charger were too bulky to be easily carried back to their dwelling. But in a corner of the barn he had noticed a dilapidated wheel barrow. He spent almost two hours straightening the axle and the handle and realigning the wheel, before loading onto it the radio and generator, and then setting off slowly over the rough terrain back to the house in the clearing.

* * * * * * * *

Jacques Friedland grew increasingly uneasy at the long absence of his friend and savior. Beckett had left him food, water, and a chamber pot, which permitted him to meet his basic needs. He was able to move his chair around the room and into the doorway of the house, so that he could look out, but he dared not venture out in his rickety chair onto the rutted terrain of the farmyard. He spent time re-examining the already inventoried contents of the cupboards and storage bins. He watched the effect of the changes in the consistently dim lighting on the sky and woods surrounding the house. He wondered about the fate of the other escaped prisoners, and tried to imagine where they were and what they were doing. He thought about Joanne back in Roussillon. Did she know they had escaped from the train? Did she know that he and Beckett were missing? How could they possibly get word out? He spent a long, lonely and uneasy day, waiting, wondering, and fretting.

A serious preoccupation for Jacques was what would become of him even if they were rescued from the farmhouse. He would certainly have to remain underground for the duration of the occupation, for years! When could he safely see Joanne again? Should he seek refuge in Switzerland? In England?

Should he try to remain in France, in hiding with other maquis in the woods of eastern France? What about the injury to his hip? Was he permanently handicapped, and therefore useless to the Resistance? His short term and long term prospects curled around each other into an obsessive question mark. Alone and immobilized, he felt increasingly overwhelmed by worry, fear and doubt. Confined to his chair and to the one room of the farmhouse, Jacques conceived the universe to be seriously limited and limiting As the sun sunk lower, and the light faded yet dimmer, so did any optimism that had survived to that point.

Finally, just as dusk began to settle in, Jacques was able to distinguish on the horizon the figure of a lone man laboriously pushing a cart across the uneven terrain. He waved and called excitedly as Sam Beckett arrived within earshot.

Before turning their attention to the repair of the radio, Beckett and Jacques worked together to prepare a hasty meal of potato and carrot soup with rice. After dinner, Jacques applied the few tools they had brought with them and others Beckett had brought back in the wheelbarrow to the repair of the radio, by the light of three candles. The screws were rusted tight, but by bathing them in olive oil, and applying steady constant pressure, Jacques was able to loosen them and open the radio's cabinet. The internal wiring was mostly intact, but there were some loose ends to whose reconnection Jacques brought his very elementary knowledge of electronics and a good deal of common sense. When he had finished, they reconnected the manual generator. Beckett turned the crank, and they watched excitedly as the vacuum tubes began to glow, and a crackling noise issued from the radio's speaker.

Jacques began to turn the dial with his attention focused on the frequency indicator, pausing over frequencies which he knew were monitored by Resistance radio operators. Mechanically, he repeated the rehearsed phrase, "Boots must be taken off every day..." several times at each promising frequency. For over thirty minutes, he patiently paused the dial, repeated the phrase, and waited for a response, before turning to the next promising frequency. Discouraged and tired, they went to bed, to begin again at dawn.

The next morning, the dawn sky hung low with heavy ponderous clouds. Perched on the stool, and peering through the small clouded windows of the farmhouse, Beckett reported down to Jacques that he found the barely perceptible horizon particularly ominous and empty.

After a quick coffee, they went back to work on the radio. For an hour, Jacques monotonously repeated the phrase, "Boots must be taken off every day..." until suddenly, a staticky voice crackled back through the speaker, "Nothing to be done." Excitedly, Jacques crowed back into the microphone, "Friedland and Beckett here; we have found refuge in a farmhouse somewhere in the woods west of Metz."

The voice responded immediately and warmly, "This is Doctor Jean-Claude Gaudeau. We have been looking for you. Give us as much information as you can about your position and surroundings. We will find you."

* * * * * * * *

Despite the optimistic words of Dr. Gaudeau, Beckett and Friedland waited a month before rescuers arrived. The escape of 144 prisoners from the train had had many positive repercussions: first of all, 144 lives saved, a burst of morale-boosting publicity for the Resistance movement, a renaissance of hope for all prisoners, and all who lived in fear of the Nazi persecutions. Moreover, the escape had brought about an immediate increase in recruits for the Resistance movement, as several of the abler escapees from the prisoner train had refused the offer of immediate transport to security in Switzerland, and had elected to remain in hiding in France to support the Resistance network. At the same time, however, there was a heavy German retaliation, beginning with a brutal crackdown on suspected Resistance fighters and their supporters throughout the Alsace and Lorraine regions. Almost daily raids on Resistance meeting places and arms caches had resulted in dozens of arrests. Resistance activity in the area became increasingly dangerous. In this environment, attempts to reach and rescue Beckett and Friedland could not be undertaken immediately.

During his short, careful radio contacts with Dr. Gaudeau, Jacques described his injury, and received guidance for treatment. Gaudeau was quite convinced, based on information provided by Beckett and Friedland, that his traumatically dislocated hip had returned to the damaged socket, and that tendon and ligament damage would begin to respond to rest and gentle therapy.

They waited a month for rescue. Almost daily

renewals of radio contact reassured them throughout the process that they were not forgotten, and that help was forthcoming. On the thirty-third day of their exile in the woods, at a time when they were just beginning to have serious worries about their food supply, they watched warily as a vehicle pulled into the front yard; it was their rescue party led by Dr. Gaudeau himself.

AFTERWORD

"What is it? What is this thing?"

In the early 1950s, Paris's Théâtre de Babylone sat inauspiciously at 38 boulevard Raspail, not too far from its busy intersections with the rue de Babylone and the rue de Sèvres, a residential and commercial area—the neighborhood for example of the Bon Marché department store—far from the intellectual and cultural focal points of the city. The theatre, perhaps because of this unfavorable location, had fallen on hard times, and in 1952 was in a state of disrepair when it was taken over by Jean-Marie Serreau, a theatrical entrepreneur, who had charged his friend Roger Blin to mount on its stage iconoclastic new works for the theatre, to be performed by talented low-profile actors willing to work for small wages in low budget but artistically challenging productions.

Thus it was that the Théâtre de Babylone, on the

night of January 23, 1953, was the stage for the world premiere of a new play, *En Attendant Godot* (*Waiting for Godot*), directed by Roger Blin, and featuring Blin himself, Jean Martin, Lucien Raimbourg, Pierre Latour, and Serge Lecointe. The author was a little known Irish writer, Samuel Beckett, who lived in Paris and who had previously published four novels.

The audience for that opening night numbered approximately two hundred curious people, many of whom were attracted by a word of mouth advertising campaign that had emphasized the revolutionary nature of the theatrical experience that awaited them. The audience was actually quite a bit larger than the director and producer had expected, and so, while many theatre-goers waited out in the street on that cold January night, the director, ushers and technicians borrowed additional chairs from a nearby café. Nine audience members, known to various degrees by the readers of this and a previous chronicle, were drawn to the theatre by reasons of personal loyalty: Richard Rosendale, Martine Lenouet, Jacques and Joanne Friedland, Suzanne Dumesnil, Félix Arnaud, Olivier and Claudine d'Anglade, and Raymond Crosatier.

To a sophisticated Paris theatre audience of the

1950s accustomed to the poetic flights of fancy or to the serious well acted naturalistic dramas of the century's established playwrights: Jean Giraudoux, Jean Cocteau, Jean Anouilh, and more recently Jean-Paul Sartre and Albert Camus, what they saw that night on the stage of the Babylone was disorienting, confusing, ambiguous, and so different from what they knew and expected, that the final curtain was greeted by most of the spectators not with thunderous or even polite applause, but with an embarrassed silence. They didn't know what they had seen, were not sure that it had in fact ended, and didn't understand.

The theatre was small and uncomfortable with folding chairs crowded together. The stage backdrop was hand sewn from several smaller pieces of cloth. The major set piece was a tree made from coat hangers and covered with crepe paper. The action consisted of the conversation of two homeless men waiting for a man named Godot, who never comes. Once in each act they are visited by a strange couple, a man and his servant, who interact with them briefly before moving on. And, at the end of each act they are visited by a boy who promises that Godot will come the following day.

After the brief curtain call, the previously

mentioned theatre-goers, along with a few other well-wishers, waited patiently in the lobby to greet personally the actors, the director and the playwright, who were invited to a reception later that night in a private room at the Closerie des Lilas. After about twenty minutes, Sam Beckett came out accompanied by the actors and Roger Blin. Following introductions, the conversation was a bit strained. The more experienced theatre-goers, Richard Rosendale, the Friedlands, and Raymond Crosatier, complimented the actors on their mastery of the play's poetic and playful language, and the director on the skillful interplay of the comic, occasionally farcical actions, and the frequently profound, disturbing, and even painful observations on human existence. No one except Richard Rosendale and Jacques Friedland really knew what to say to Beckett, except to congratulate him on the successful opening night of a very difficult play. Richard and Jacques in a few brief words let him know that they understood and recognized, and were deeply moved by what they had seen. Beckett acknowledged and appreciated their sincere homage, but also understood and appreciated the malaise of the others. He had been counting on that.

It was Olivier and Claudine d'Anglade who had organized the after theatre party. Olivier had remained in government service following the war, in the Interior Ministry of the Gaullist cabinet. As soon as Claudine had returned from her exile in London, they had been able to re-establish the connections which had in the 1930s made them one of the most sought after couples in Paris's highest social circles. Olivier retired from government service in 1950, but remained active in political circles where his wit, wisdom, and reputation for heroism during the war were recognized and appreciated. He wore proudly the decorations he had received for his service to the Resistance.

When Richard Rosendale had written to him with advance notice of the opening of Beckett's play, d'Anglade had eagerly proposed that the opening would present a splendid opportunity to bring back together, after nearly ten years, several of the actors in one of the Resistance's most notable strikes against the German death camp transportation network, the successful escape on June 13, 1943, of 144 prisoners on their way to Nazi extermination camps in Poland.

In the immediate aftermath of his and Beckett's rescue from the abandoned farmhouse in July,

1943, Jacques Friedland had taken refuge in the French Alps in the village of Villars de Lans, and had remained there until the end of the war, first of all waiting for his injured hip to heal, and then contributing actively to the work of Resistance units in the area, who rescued and hid young Jewish children from throughout occupied France, who were given refuge in farms in the Alps. Joanne was able to join him there late in 1943. Jacques and Joanne had returned to Roussillon at the end of the war, but then moved back to Paris in the fall of 1947, following the retirement of Joanne's cousin, Alfred Pons, who had been managing their gallery on the rue de Seine. Félix Arnaud, Richard Rosendale and Sam Beckett had spent the remaining war years in Roussillon, continuing to support the Resistance movement, Beckett had returned to Paris immediately after the war, and the Rosendales at the same time as the Friedlands in 1947. Arnaud was living in Nice where he was a professor at the University, and had come up to Paris for the theatre opening.

The reception at the Closerie des Lilas began rather awkwardly. The Rosendales, Sam Beckett and Suzanne Dumesnil, and the Friedlands had remained in close contact in the ten years since the war. But Sam Beckett had never met d'Anglade—although he owed his life to him. The others had not seen d'Anglade since the war, and they had never met his wife Claudine. But as soon as they had all arrived and begun sipping on the champagne that was waiting for them, d'Anglade made a brief speech, and then he and Claudine moved among them, conversing comfortably and familiarly in a way that put everyone at ease.

D'Anglade reminisced with the Rosendales and the Friedlands about their time together in Vence before the war, and then of course with them, Arnaud, and Beckett about the events of June 1943 that had brought them together again. Beckett was especially curious to learn details about d'Anglade's role in creating the arrest warrant for *Murphy*, which had permitted him to board the train from Drancy. D'Anglade explained how he had been able to do that with the help of Joseph Brunot, and gave them all information they hadn't previously known about the input from railroad workers within the Resistance network that had been instrumental in the formulation of the escape plan. He also told them of Louis Darquier's and Alois Brunner's unwitting contributions of information. Then he surprised them all by announcing mysteriously,

"Did you know, Mr. Beckett, that you were not the only fake prisoner in car number 16?"

Both Beckett and Friedland were intrigued. "Another fake prisoner?"

"Didn't any of the others strike you as being somewhat out of the ordinary?"

Beckett answered, "There was the big fellow, Goldberg was his name."

"Exactly," answered d'Anglade. "That was the name he assumed in order to infiltrate the prisoner train."

"He wasn't a real prisoner either?"

"No, in fact he was before the war one of France's brightest police inspectors. Immediately following the occupation, he joined the Paris Resistance Council. His remarkable physical and mental talents contributed to the success of many of our initiatives against the Germans in the Paris region. He and I were very close."

Beckett was surprised, "You thought we needed help?"

"Yes, please forgive me, I thought you might need an extra pair of hands, and an extra pair of eyes. Remember, I had never met you. I knew that Arnaud and Rosendale possessed the judgment, physical prowess, and courage to manage the escape from car number 18. But I was a bit reluctant to entrust the escape of the seventy prisoners from car number 16 to Jacques Friedland and an Irish novelist whom I had never met. I sent the so-called Goldberg along for security. I thought you should know. Please forgive me if I slighted you. I learned later that it was for the most part an unnecessary precaution. You and Jacques clearly mastered the situation in the train car. But when you two became separated in the march from the prison to the train car, you might not have gotten back together without his intervention."

"The man who had grabbed Jacques and was gesturing indiscreetly! I had completely forgotten about that. That was the same Goldberg?"

"Exactly."

"No, I understand perfectly your prudence. And we might not have managed without him. Though it was in consequence of his size that the floor opening was damaged, Jacques was injured, and we spent a month in that abandoned farm."

D'Anglade nodded. "That is regrettable."

Beckett smiled, "Not necessarily."

"Why do you say that?"

"It turned out to be one of the most intense experiences of my life. We were exhilarated to learn from our short radio communications with the Resistance network of the successful escape of all of the prisoners from the two cars. At the same time, Jacques and I had to deal with our own survival in the difficult context of his injury. But then there was day after day of monotonous leisure, the time to think and reflect, and much to think and reflect about. There was the remarkable adventure of our escape through the water and mud, and the very strange environment in which we found ourselves, with Jacques confined to the wheel chair, and me a slave to his needs, committed as I was to his survival. And then, while we waited for rescue, there were our conversations, our attempts to fill the void of our time with words, ideas, and stories. That experience continues to feed my poor imagination."

At this point Richard Rosendale chimed in, "As we saw on stage this evening."

Beckett merely smiled. Richard, sensing that Beckett had said perhaps more than he intended, went on, "Tell us more, d'Anglade, about the other fake prisoner. What is his real name?"

D'Anglade laughed heartily. "He was and is now again Inspector Jean-Luc Saccard of the National Police."

Richard gasped, "Is he not the man..."

D'Anglade interrupted him, "Yes, indeed, the man whose dogged integrity and police skills led to my downfall in 1937."

"And you subsequently became close colleagues in the Resistance?"

"And lifelong friends. Yes, Richard, life has its ironic twists. Saccard, a modest and unassuming man, with talent, determination and a desire only to do good, first of all causes my arrest and disgrace; and then, years later, working with me as a close ally, he is directly responsible for the terrible injury suffered by Jacques Friedland, which nearly causes the capture or death of Beckett and Friedland. And now we learn that this accident has also a redemptive quality. I can't wait to tell him."

Richard turned to Beckett, "I couldn't help sensing while watching your two clowns on stage tonight, that they have evolved quite a bit from what you had told us about them that night in June of '43 when we were driving up to Gap to rescue Jacques. Is that evolution related to the Saccard effect?"

Beckett paused thoughtfully for quite a while and then answered, "I have always been preoccupied by the pathetic trajectory of the human experience: our physical frailty, our depravity, our vulnerability, our basic inability to understand what we are doing here, our destiny to seek and to fail to find. But our shared adventure in the spring of '43, from its daunting start with Jacques' arrest in Apt to its long drawn out conclusion in the abandoned farmhouse, put everything in a new perspective: We learned that some human calculations are accurate and useful. Some human ambitions can succeed. Humanity can surpass its limits. For every wicked initiative, there may be a good counterpoint. We can perhaps prevail. Much of that I discovered through our experience of the rescue mission, and through the opportunity that Jacques and I were given to reflect on it during the long days we spent in the wilderness. So yes, the Saccard effect contributes to what you saw and heard on stage tonight."

"I will continue to be fascinated by pathetic creatures who fall victim to their physical and mental limits, and to the indifference of an uncaring environment. People will get old, get sick, weaken, and lose their wits. But they will continue to...continue to...the only word I come up with to describe what they will continue to do is play. And I mean play as in childish activity, but also as in a theatre, and as in the metaphoric sense of 'play out,' that is to fulfill something that is prescribed for them. They will play their roles."

At this point, Raymond Crosatier, who had said little in the course of the evening, came over and joined the group with Samuel Beckett, Richard Rosendale and d'Anglade, pen and moleskin notebook in hand. "I overheard, Mr. Beckett, what you were just saying about the role of the escape adventure in the evolution of your writing. Do you expect to ever address the experience directly? To write a narrative of it."

"No, never," he answered with a smile. "That is a task for a journalist. My gift to you, Mr. Crosatier."

EDUCATING ANDREW
By Virginia Lanier Biasotto

The strongest bond in the animal kingdom is mother and offspring.

When something threatens, the mother instinctively acts to protect. The story of Andrew is a human example, and the enemy was one of our most revered institutions: the public school.

For most children, the beginning of school is a time of anticipation and excitement. New clothes and supplies are purchased. A preliminary visit to the classroom sets the stage for the promise, "This is where you will learn to read." For Andrew, the reading part didn't happen. For seven years solutions were sought, found and rejected. The printed page remained a mystery. The effects of his failure to read were dire. Andrew's love of life had been taken away, and his parents and teachers were helpless to do anything about it.

Paperback, 132 pages
5.5" x 8.5"
ISBN 1-4241-0171-9

When it appeared that Andrew would remain illiterate as he entered junior high school, a door opened that would change his life and that of his mother forever.

About the author:

VIRGINIA (GINGER) LANIER BIASOTTO is a native of Delaware and a graduate of the University of Delaware (1959). She is the founder of Reading ASSIST® Institute and the author of ten Reading ASSIST® text books. In 2005, Virginia received Delaware's Jefferson Award for Public Service for her contribution to literacy. She and her husband, Lawrence, are semi-retired and spend half of each year in Wilmington, Delaware, close to children, grandchildren and mothers, and the other half in Palm City, Florida.

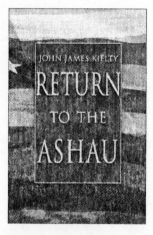

THE SEED OF OMEGA
By Eugene Ettlinger

The Seed of Omega depicts the molding of rural Palestine from the windblown nomadic land of weeds and sand into a Mecca in the Middle East. The land was populated by assimilation through different cultures, which includes an ethnic invasion after the soil had been tilled. A greater understanding of political power through favored in-migration status shows the melding of a select society. The power brokers governing the land became subservient to the will of neighboring nations in exchange for the production of oil. The cast is composed of variations of the Middle Eastern Arab people, the power brokers of the British Empire and the exiles from hostile nations the world over.

Paperback, 511 pages
6" x 9"

ISBN 1-4137-8882-3

The diversity of characters represents different walks of life to be filled by the shoes of the reader. They fought for survival and a love for one another. They were dedicated to the building of a society while struggling to implement a diverse nation running from a past life simply to find a place in which to be. Their fears are offset by the courage to survive in the creation of a nation.

About the author:

A native New Yorker and Fordham University graduate, Gene Ettlinger performed graduate studies in the field of sociology. Gene's dedication is in the development of community life. Growing up in the mixing bowl of ethnic diversity led to his keen interest in the alienation of unskilled workers. Gene is a pilot, skier, skilled boating enthusiast, and an accomplished artist. He currently resides in New York and Florida.

Also available from PublishAmerica

SIOBHAN
An AI's Adventure
By Emma L. Haynes

Siobhan: An AI's Adventure is a story
that follows an android from his creation
to his death. His most important mission
is to pilot a colony ship filled with one
hundred humans to a new planet, where
he is to become a simple computer. A
colonist tries to kill Siobhan before they
land at their destination. This disruption
causes the colony ship to shoot past the
desired planet and crash land on a planet
of an advanced race. Siobhan and only
three humans survive. Fighting off attacks
from the locals, Siobhan gets them off the
planet.

Paperback, 176 pages
5.5" x 8.5"
ISBN 978-1-60749-130-9

About the author:

Emma L. Haynes lives in North Pole, Alaska. She is married to an
Army soldier and has one son. Through the years, she has enjoyed
writing poetry, science fiction, fantasy, and historical fiction. She plans
to travel the world when she gets the chance. She has one book
published entitled *Poems from the Heart*. Visit her website at
www.EmmaLHaynes.com.

Available to all bookstores nationwide.
www.publishamerica.com